IN

FOREIGN

PARTS

art & stories by

ELISABETH STEVENS

BIRCH
BROOK
PRESS

First edition

Library of Congress Catalog Number: 97-074379

ISBN: 0-913559-39-3

Etchings by the author, Elisabeth Stevens

Certain of these stories have appeared or will be appearing in the following publications: *Anima, Confrontation, Late Knocking, Lite Circle, The Potomac Review.*

Typeset and printed letterpress at
     Birch Brook Press
     PO Box 81
     Delhi, NY 13753

Write for free catalog of books and art.

In
Foreign
Parts

This is nothing but dreaming . . .
Ulalume, Edgar Allan Poe

What bitter knowledge we gain
from traveling!
Le Voyage, Charles Baudelaire

Stories   Art

ABOUT THE AUTHOR

A fiction writer, poet, artist and journalist, Elisabeth Stevens is the author of six books. Her collections of short fiction are: *In Foreign Parts*, Birch Brook Press, 1997; *Horse & Cart: Stories From the Country*, Wineberry Press, 1990; *Fire & Water: Six Stories*, Perivale Press, 1983. Her poetry collections are: *The Night Lover*, Birch Brook Press, 1995; *Children of Dust: Portraits & Preludes*, The New Poets Series, 1983. *Elisabeth Stevens' Guide to Baltimore's Inner Harbor* was published in 1981. A resident of Baltimore, she has won fiction awards from *The Maryland Poetry Review, Lite Circle* and *The Antietam Review* and a drama award from The Baltimore Writers' Alliance.

As a journalist, she has written many articles, art reviews and book reviews. She is a former art critic of *The Washington Post, The Wall Street Journal, The Trenton Times*, and most recently, *The Baltimore Sun*.

><=<

ABOUT THE BOOK

In Foreign Parts was typeset in metal by hand in 11 pt. Kennerley, a font designed by Frederic W. Goudy, and was printed letterpress on a V-45 Miehle Vertical, with color work produced on a hand-delivery Chandler & Price platen press. Author's etchings were printed from wood-mounted metal engravings. Text stock is 80 lb. Mohawk Vellum, Cream White. Cover stock is Tuscan Antique.

◦━ INTRODUCTION ━◦

By DAVID KRIEBEL

Prior to meeting Elisabeth Stevens, I had developed an admiration for her work, both poetry and prose, and had published her illustrated story *The Dance*. That admiration has grown through the years—through her writings in print, her artwork, and her readings. Ms. Stevens' readings are lively and energized with vivid characterization, as if you are listening to a stage play. You feel her presence in the world she creates, not as a character, but as a fellow reader, guiding you into the world of her imagination.

And what an imagination it is! Her stories range from the innocent and childlike to the chilling and macabre, but they are all touched with the same originality. She has written convincingly from every viewpoint and, as the nine stories in this volume attest, she always manages to find the best voice for the situation. Her stories are fiction, but they ring true, causing one to wonder whether or not they have a basis in fact.

In Foreign Parts is a masterful collection of the author's most bizarre and often disturbing pieces, and it is aptly titled. Reading these stories, one feels a true sense of being in unfamiliar territory, a trespasser in the more shadowy regions of the imagination. This is the real stuff, more horrific than any Wes Craven motion picture, because it is executed by an artist with an insight into the dark side of the soul, a writer who need not rely on gory effects to achieve her ends.

In that, it is reminiscent of the best of Roald Dahl or Robert Bloch. Like those writers, Ms. Stevens has a sense of the absurd and knows that we fear those things we find strange and in violation of the norms established by America's cult of the above-average. She shocks us not by being crude and stark, but by taking what we know of life and standing it on its head, until our own imagination slips its moorings and is carried into an ocean of uncertainty, with the narrative authority of the writer our only compass.

Certainly not all of these stories could fairly be called "horror." I doubt Ms. Stevens uses that word to describe what she writes. Yet these are what fans of that genre yearn for when they decry the lack of subtlety in today's books and movies, the substitution of gross description and depiction for haunting dread. The stories herein are haunted, haunted by the spectre of our own mortality. They are not pulp fiction, but meditations on what it means to be human, with the need to make sense of an apparently capricious and uncaring world. These stories, bizarre as they may seem on the surface, are merely dramatizations of life, the real world as seen through a funhouse mirror. The distortions have the power to horrify us only because they are so close to the reality we know...or think we know.

A word must be said here about the execution of these stories. They are almost painterly in their detail: sketched, rather than written. This doubtless stems from Ms. Stevens' considerable talent in the visual media, evidenced by the "etchings" which accompany and illuminate these works, and printed from engravings in this letterpress edition. Her care in selecting the elements of each piece and her attention to minute detail reveal the hand of a master crafts-woman. Another element that is linked to the visual impact of the stories is lyricism. These stories, like lyric poems, do not see time as a sequence, but an occasion for meaning. There is continual repetition and return, whether embodied in memories, fantasies, or the presence of the dead who have somehow manifested in the present. These stories also resemble poems in that every word counts. Nothing is wasted here.

At the same time these stories are more than just very well-done tales of the bizarre. They are musings on human nature, sometimes expressed with dark satire ("The Pit"), sometimes with philosophical speculation ("In Foreign Parts"), sometimes with psychological portraiture ("I Told You So"). Our nature is defined, in part, by our mortality. The knowledge that death awaits us haunts both our lives and these stories, and Ms. Stevens is capable of presenting it in its most horrifying form (see "Daddy Cerements," or "The Box"). However, she balances that knowledge with wonder, hinting that death may not, after all, be the end.

I know you will enjoy this collection and hope you will continue to seek out Ms. Stevens' work, both poetry and prose. If you do, you will discover a writer and artist with a rich imagination, a gift for characterization, and most of all, with the ability to make you think.

⇌ In Foreign Parts ⇌

THE TAPE RECORDING

"I shouldn't tell you this. First of all, no one will believe me.
Even if you do get out and write your story, it will be too late to—
"No, when I cough like that don't try to help me. Just open
the transept windows. The guns in the east, I'm used to them. It's
the sun sinking in the west that will kill all of us—and you—so
young and so pale. A man becomes accustomed to it, but this isn't a
woman's climate. You've only been here three days. After a while
you'll discover....
"Yes, give me the medicine. It's only a palliative, but I'll take
it. Before it makes me sleep, I must tell you how it all happened."

The Guidebook

The Capital stands 230 feet above sea level on a small western
affluent. The fertility of the land is demonstrated by the abundance
of sheep, ivory and ostrich feathers. The inhabitants are noted for
their muscular development and their Herculean frames. They believe
in the Transmigration of Souls.

THE TAPE RECORDING

"Yes, you must sit down. It's a long tale like no other. That old
missionary prayer stool will do nicely. Draw it close. The drug slows
the heart. I can barely whisper. Your red hair—spun threads of
copper—I can see the sun setting in the hills through the curls at

your face. The child's hair was that very color. No matter now—unless someone should take it to mind to think—

"Your machine is in order? Good. I won't live to tell my story twice.

"Before all this began, I was an ordinary person—a plain soul in a plain place, but nobody's fool. I was young then, not an old man. Yes, 40 *is* old in this impossible place. If you had told me then I'd end up *here*—dying of a disease that doesn't have a name—I wouldn't have believed you.

"Like you, I was a journalist—but not an American or a foreign correspondent. I was entirely local—an English scrivener. I had a regular column called 'Tidbits.' My restaurant reviews and recipes had a following. I lived well, in a modest way. I ate well.

"Then, long a bachelor, I married for love. Ten months later, Brigid gave birth. The child had no arms. Instead—three legs radiating out of its belly. The creature resembled a wheel. It lived. My wife died.

"Three days later, I took the little beast home. Not for long though. I stopped only to pack a suitcase. There had been an announcement opposite the obituary page in the paper—a promotional fare, a struggling airline. I purchased a ticket."

The Guidebook

Rising from remote, wave-swept expanses far to the west, the city and its faubourgs are ringed by short ranges. The plateau escarpments turn to towering peaks in the wild and distant lands where the sun rises. Most of the mountains there have received the names of their explorers.

In the civilised zone conditions are far more favorable to herbaceous than to arboreal vegetation. Both the climate and the relief of the land are unfavorable to the development of large water courses.

THE TAPE RECORDING

"No, you didn't wake me. I doze and come to again—that's the way the drug works. Before this complex was appropriated by the late government as the main hospital—if you can still call it that, the last doctor died yesterday—this structure was a Christian sanctuary. When I open my eyes, I see saints in the ceiling—and behind them, where the paint is peeling, enormous images from the days before the missionaries when this was a pagan temple.

"We're dining on rice—but where in the world did you find it? There hasn't been any in the markets since The Blue forces carried the King away to the mountains. It looks so white, so delicious, and the fragrance of the tea is heavenly. Give me only a little. I must complete my narrative. If their soldiers return to the city tomorrow, we shall not be sipping tea at twilight.

"I went straight to the airport, as I was telling you. As I left the apartment, I wrapped the child in my wife's wedding dress covered by a large blanket—an awkward bundle. Then I merely turned the key in the door, leaving everything as it was—no forwarding address.

"As I said, I'd always been a plain fellow—did my job, took my wages. I'm not sure what I had in mind when I boarded the plane with my wailing, white lace shrouded burden. Perhaps it was to find an obscure and kindly woman whom I would set up as generously as I could—so that she would keep the child.

"Perhaps—it was one of those things you don't fully consider, I thought I could accomplish it all in a week or a weekend—and go back and simply take up my life the way it had been before I fell in love.

"Instead, from the very moment I went down the rickety steps they rolled up to the plane and headed toward the arched, cavernous ruin they called the airport with my wailing, urine-soaked charge, it seemed I was being drawn down into a *cul de sac* from which there was no way up.

"It happened immediately, as I was waiting for my luggage. Of course I was trying to quiet the little beast, and somehow, the wrappings slipped away. Someone—there were all sorts crowded beyond the barrier, pushing, gesticulating, calling to the passengers— must have seen. I remember hearing a woman scream.

"Then the luggage was brought out. Mine was cumbersome— mostly infant equipment, and in the confusion of getting it, I set the creature at the side on a bench. When I returned, there was only the soiled, wadded wedding dress. The child and the blanket were gone."

The Guidebook

The Boulevard du Nord winds from the new airfield to La Porte de Saint Paul. The palms that once lined the avenue were cut down in the great conflict. The boulevard has lately been extended to the east by an autobahn. The autobahn is 35 km. long. It has no toll barriers. It leads nowhere.

THE TAPE RECORDING

"No, don't try to feed me. In my state, two teaspoonfulls is a banquet. Save the rest. You may need it. Let me continue.

"Searching for the child, I rushed into the crowd. There were other swaddled infants—but not my three-spoked red pate. Eventually, I gathered my things together. In this country, there are greater oddities than a man with an empty perambulator.

"When I got to the hotel, I ate. When I went to bed, I slept."

The Guidebook

The Alte Bahnhof (1889) stands within La Porte de Saint Paul. Most of the Egyptianizing figures that originally adorned the terminal's elaborate facade are missing. The Bahnhof faces the Schlossplatz, which has long contained the Great Market.

Four blocks to the south by way of Le Boulevard des Hommes, the fashionable quarter begins. There, Le Grand Hotel, a replica, it is believed, of one of the finest places in Paris, faces Les Jardins de la Jeunesse. This spacious, rectangular park is traversed by angular, intersecting paths, all leading to La Fontaine de la Jeunesse, said to be the center point of the city. The large, circular fountain is adorned with life-sized statues of the Muses. It is now dry.

THE TAPE RECORDING

"The next day, I considered notifying the authorities. I didn't want to attract attention, so I decided against it. I determined to wait it out, in case whoever had taken the three-legger should contact me, ask for ransom, or—even worse—report what I had come to do.

"Seeing I wouldn't be able to return home as I had planned, I wrote a friend and asked him to store what was in my flat. I sent him the key.

"Then, living like a tourist of means, I found an old guidebook and explored the city."

The Guidebook

Le Musee de l'Homme contains ancient tablets, chiefly relating to music and cookery. A few costumes and utensils survive from ancient religious practices, the memory of which is buried in oblivion.

It is believed that haurispachy was once practiced in the mountains of the east with sheep and other animals. Aged informants have described ghastly customs connected with these rites, which honored a deformed and now forgotten god of the sun.

THE TAPE RECORDING

"As I said, I became a tourist. After some days, I exhausted the attractions of the city. My funds were running short, yet I was determined to wait for word about the child. After a time, I rented a room and took a clerk's job at an Indian company that was importing machine parts in a roundabout way from Japan. They needed someone to write purchase orders and render bills.

"It went on that way for some time. There were a few letters from my friend at home, then nothing. Without intending to, I began a new life.

"I took up with one of the women in the office—a plain creature, but she was kind to me. I had someone to stroll with in the evenings."

The Guidebook

At the foot of the incline that commences in the residential district south of the Royal Palace, is the Cimetere des Anges. Access is by steps at the western end of La Rue des Artistes.

The mound at the right contains remnants of ancient ruins. Many of the older monuments have been lost. Along the main allee, one finds the tombs of General Von Seiler, the philosopher Le Moyne, and the actress Elizabeth Renaldi.

The old charnel house still stands far at the left, beyond the evergreens. It is filled with rubbish.

THE TAPE RECORDING

"Months passed. In this country, time lacks the crispness of progression—the snap of tearing a page off the calendar. The rains, the heat, the rains, the heat. That's all you notice. Even day and night don't seem particularly different. The sun is always there—sometimes obscured by brown shadows, sometimes not.

"Although I'd been waiting for it, the letter came as a surprise.

By then, more than a year had passed. My child, my wife, the place I had come from scarcely seemed real to me.

"The letter—it had been mailed in the mountains—had no return address. That didn't matter. There's no answer to a drawing. Just a circle and a few lines pencilled in red. By then, I knew what the three-pronged thing was called. The triskelion.

"It was odd—once I had the letter—that I didn't return to England. I had accomplished what I had come for. I knew they were raising the child. Yet—did I wish to see my little creature again?—I stayed.

"In the meantime, my woman sickened. She died six months ago of the thing that's taking me. It was at that time that the insurgency began—first in a hamlet, far to the east, then spreading like wildfire, everywhere.

"The King was old, the situation worsened. Many fled the country in fear. Shipments were disrupted, food became scarce. In the midst of it—how one clings to habit—I went on in the same way like a martinet.

"My path to and from work was unvarying. Each morning at the same hour, I passed the high gates of the Royal Palace."

The Guidebook

The Royal Palace bespeaks a disposition to indolent enjoyments. The modern section is situated beside La Cour des Lions with its great gates. Within this compound reside the despotic and unfettered descendants of the immemorial royal line. The King is the adjudicator of an absurd and drastic penal code, the primate of bloody and bar-baric forms of worship.

All that remains of the original courts and fountains far to the rear—pleasure gardens once so celebrated, so universally known, are scattered, rough-hewn stones. The ruins are said to contain porcupine quills; the cavities are inhabited by bats and owls.

THE TAPE RECORDING

"One morning though, my fixed course was interrupted. At the very gates, an old woman crossed my path. At first, I took her for a beggar. Then, she forced a wad of paper into my palm.

"The woman—I wondered later if she was the child's nurse—disappeared. When I smoothed out what she had given me I saw it was an airline schedule—a list of planes going home.

"That evening, I returned home as usual. For many nights, I had been toying with a stamp collection I'd been forming. The three-legged sun figure, I had learned, appeared on issues going back for many years.

"I set the schedule aside, but it was obvious, wasn't it? They wanted me to leave. I hadn't made a move in their direction, but my mere presence was an obstacle. The father of a god—if mortal—is in the way. Such a man must disappear into the dimness of history—or rise to a remote pantheon like the signs in the ceiling above us."

The Guidebook

To the south, at the end of La Rue des Panoramas, is the old sacred center, which was transformed after the great conflict into a modern, sanitary hospital. The chambers adjoining the cloisters accommodate administrative offices, and the former chapel boasts more than thirty beds.

The walls of the time-honored sanctuary were adorned with sacred images by the missionary fathers. Many have admired the brilliance and size of their painted conceptions.

THE TAPE RECORDING

"Yes, I'll take tea, but only a swallow—solid food no longer interests me.

"To conclude, in the last weeks before they brought me here, I was ill and alone. I became obsessed with the triskelion. I found one on a Greek vase in a neglected corner of the museum. I located several on broken stones in the oldest section of the cemetery. There was even a small incision in the center of La Fontaine de la Jeunesse.

"In the market, I caught sight of the sign scratched in chalk on the side of a booth, and one day, sipping coffee in a cafe, I saw the mark tattooed on the back of a man's hand.

"Oddly—it may have been my illness—I began to suspect that the guidebook was entirely misleading, that it concealed more than it illustrated. I realized that the city was roughly circular—and that there were three streets radiating from La Fontaine de la Jeunesse. I began to suspect that—

"Everything, in short, began to strike me as decaying, insubstantial. It was the triskelion—of which my poor child was the merest mirror fragment—that was puissant, overpowering.

"Yes, of course you're tired, it's been dark for hours. I've been rambling, surely. We'll continue in the morning. This country takes more from one than you may expect. In the end, it takes everything."

THE REPORTER'S NOTEBOOK

12:30 a.m.: The Englishman became feverish as the evening progressed. His knowledge of the new cult is fragmentary, hypothetical. I called the old nurse to care for him, but no one came.

The Guidebook

The unsettled section beyond the hospital contains the remains of ancient ceremonial structures. Among the ruins, a worn path of stones winding beyond the city's southern limits leads to a sacred well.

The well, it is said, still gushes water in certain seasons. On such occasions, natives flock to the place for ceremonial remembrances of souls of the dead. Strange offerings encircle branches bending above moist stones.

THE TAPE RECORDING

"Oh no, I've been awake since sunrise, contemplating the ceiling. This is the equinox, you know, and when the sun rose, it shone through that round window, illuminating the dome like a spotlight. Behind the eyes of the huge, flaking head of Christ above me is the three-legged sign. I saw it the day they brought me here, although no one else had noticed. There were other patients then— all since have died. Now—perchance more paint is falling—it is clearer by the hour.

"Last night, my rest was interrupted. You slept well?

"I meant to warn you about that. Those cries from the crypt are not worth investigating. It could be a lamb. Pay no mind to it. The old King was imprisoned there only a few hours—then they carried him far away. They may have left the animal for a future sacrifice. In any case, no one has the key.

"Oh yes, the lamb could stand for the King in their minds— they believe in the transmigration of souls. If the King has since died, as some have told you, then they will sacrifice the lamb when they return. Afterwards, they examine the liver for signs. It's called haurispachy, but I'm no expert. I've dealt with liver for dinner with onions—not divination.

"No tea today. When one is reposing in death's arms, sustenance is less appealing than certain imaginings. Last night, for instance, I could have sworn that there were postulants on the path to the well. Among them, it seemed, I heard my poor child singing in a high, whining, infantile way."

The Song of the Three-Legged Child

I am the sun
I am the one.

My three legs run
The circle of gold.

THE TAPE RECORDING

"The song—no more than a figment of a fever, you understand, put me in mind of something else.

"At first, I fancied they had brought my child to bid me good-bye. Then, as the footsteps faded and the voice grew faint, it struck me that whatever one does—the child I married to father, the story you braved your way here to write—can completely outstrip us. What will be done with my three legger—or even with your narra-tive—is out of our control.

"Therefore, there's always the danger—as I see it—of being consumed by the very thing you wished or worked for. At that juncture, of course, it's too late to claim: this is not what I intended.

"There's a certain justice in such an ending—and yet—"

WIRE SERVICE REPORT:

THE STREETS OF THE CAPITAL WERE QUIET LAST NIGHT, BUT SOURCES AT THE NOW NEARLY ABANDONED CAPITAL WHERE THE OLD RULER DISAPPEARED DURING HARD FIGHTING LAST WEEK SAID AN ATTACK FROM THE MOUNTAINS WAS ANTICIPATED WITHIN 24 HOURS. LAST NIGHT, THE INSURGENTS CELE-

BRATED AN EQUINOXIAL SUN FESTIVAL.
THE FESTIVAL, IT IS BELIEVED, WAS
CENTERED ON A MYSTERIOUS NEW CULT
THAT HAS ARISEN RECENTLY IN CON-
JUNCTION WITH A THREE-LEGGED CHILD.

THE TAPE RECORDING

"No, when I cough like that I don't want water. If you have liquor, give it to me now. The time has come.

"Yes, that's better. Let me lie back. In the rim of the dome, there is a lamb. He is encircled with gold cups—overflowing . . . spilling red. . . .

"I am cold. Clasp my hands. This is the end. I will be remembered, if at all, as the father of—

"You must take care. Avoid the crypt. Your hair . . . remember . . . is as red as the child's. . . ."

THE REPORTER'S NOTEBOOK

1 p.m.: The Englishman is gone. He died peacefully. The nurse knows.

The moaning has begun again. I am going to visit the crypt.

WIRE SERVICE REPORT:

MOUNTAIN-BASED INSURGENTS SWEPT
THROUGH THE CAPITAL YESTESDAY AFTER-
NOON WITHOUT ENCOUNTERING RESIS-
TANCE. THE STREETS AND PARKS ARE
ABANDONED, ALTHOUGH A FEW SURVIVORS
HAVE BEEN REPORTED IN THE HOSPITAL

SECTOR. AN ENGLISHMAN DIED THERE
YESTERDAY. NEARBY, IN AN OLD CRYPT,
A LAMB WAS RITUALLY DISMEMBERED.
THE BLUE FORCES ARE NOW REGROUP-
ING TWENTY MILES TO THE EAST. THEY
ARE SAID TO HAVE WITH THEM A 23 YEAR
OLD HOSTAGE, AN AMERICAN WOMAN
CORRESPONDENT. THE HOSTAGE, CERTAIN
NATIVES REPORT, IS THE RED-HEADED
MOTHER OF THE RED-HEADED, THREE-
LEGGED CHILD.
THERE IS NO FURTHER INFORMATION.

EDITORS' NOTE

The tape recordings, guidebook selections and other materials
came into our hands only recently at auction in London. These
materials, brought home by unknown hands, were contained in a
manilla envelope bearing the imprint of an American newspaper,
except for the final report. This item was generously provided by a
leading wire service from its files.

As inquiries now directed to Blues in power have gone unans-
wered, the American woman who disappeared many months ago is
presumed lost. The three-legged child, however, is said to be alive
and well, and growing.

The Box

Mommy and Daddy go out a lot. When they go, Aunt comes.
Aunt is big, almost as big as Daddy. There is a hair on her chin
that prickles when she kisses good-night.

I am a good boy. Mommy told me. Toys on the floor, toys by
the door, she loves me.

Aunt loves me. But Aunt is different. She doesn't love me if I
don't put my toys in the box.

The box is big. It is beside my bed. Mommy calls it a chest.
There are four feet on it. The feet have claws. But they don't scratch.

The box has a key, but Daddy says not to lock it because the
box is old. Sometimes the top sticks. If the key got lost, we might
never be able to open the box again.

Once, Daddy helped me put all my soldiers and spacemen away.
It was Christmas. That was when Aunt wasn't here.

Now Aunt is here. She came in the morning. She will be here
tomorrow when I wake up. Mommy told me.

Aunt is finishing her supper. I am to play quietly until she
comes to put me in. I am to put my toys away.

Aunt doesn't know about the Igs. I told Mommy once. It was
in the middle of the night. I called for her, and she came and kissed
them away. They weren't the Igs any more—just shadows on the
wall.

When Aunt is here at night—don't tell her, even Mommy
doesn't know—*I take my toys out of the box again.*

I do it after she goes to sleep. Aunt sleeps a long time. Sometimes I have to go and get my own cereal out. Before she wakes up,
I put the toys away again.

When I get them out at night, the soldiers and spacemen protect me. The bark dog with the red collar is good too, but I keep him very quiet. The farm animals are all right. But they're small.

The Igs are big. They move very fast. They can jump on you from behind and put their long black feathery tails around your neck.

Aunt is coming. I hear her shoes in the hall. She is humming to herself. She is big in the doorway. I don't see the hall light any more. She fills up the room. She smells like sand.

I get into bed myself. I pull the covers way up before she comes to kiss.

Aunt goes to the box. She stops there and does something. She goes to the bureau. "You are a good boy," she says, "you put all your toys away."

She turns out the light. Her shoes go down the hall.

The Igs are getting ready. They are very quiet about it. They only move a little at first—along the baseboards and in the corner beside the closet.

Just as quietly, I pull the covers back. I get up, I go to the box. The top is stuck.

The hall light is still on. I see what the matter is. Aunt has taken the key.

No. She has put it on the bureau. I can reach it.

The key has never been out of the lock before. It does not know how to go back in. The Igs are out. They have voices this time. I hear them whispering.

I push the key. It works. My box is open but the Igs are ahead of me. They are all moving together—very fast. It is too late to take out my toys. The Igs are big—bigger than Aunt.

The Igs are all leaving the walls at once. They try to get the key. They have heavy fingers. Their tails are sticky. They want to wrap them around my neck.

I don't let them. Instead, I boost myself up. I climb into the box. The soldiers and the spacemen and the dog and the farm animals are waiting for me. The lid comes down shut. The Igs are outside. They can't get in.

I am all right. I have the key.

⊨ The Pit ⊨

Every day I ask why they are digging the pit, but no one tells me.

It began yesterday. It began the day before. It began a week ago or more down the hill from our development.

Our development is row houses strung out down the hill in blocks of four. Then there's the chain link fence. The pit is down there beside the tracks. On the other side of the tracks is the old park—the falling down dock and the boat yard where people have left boats and never come back for them.

Beyond the boat yard is the bay, and beyond the bay is the city. When I get up in the morning, I see white smoke from the trains, and behind it, black smoke from the big buildings. Because we are near the water, gulls circle in the smoke.

Our house—we moved here from the apartment after the baby came—has three windows in the back. I can see the pit from all of them—downstairs, from the kitchen window by the table where we eat, and upstairs, from the window in the bedroom beside the bed and from the window in the bathroom over the tub.

I was standing in the shower when I saw the pit for the first time. I had my hand between my legs, parting the lips, washing. Reddish, soapy water was running down my thighs. In the ruffle-edged triangle where the green waterproof curtains didn't meet, I saw two men dressed in brown. One was at the left of the little furrow they had made at the base of the hillside, one was at the right. They were tapping into the earth with picks. What they had exposed was rust colored—like blood on the ragged edge of a wound.

The next morning I got up when Ronnie was still sleeping. He works the night shift. From between the blue bedroom curtains, I saw the cut had become a rectangle. Four men were digging instead of two, and they were in the pit up to their shoulders.

I closed the curtains then so the sun wouldn't get in Ronnie's face. Later, when he'd had his dinner and gone to work and the baby was asleep in her crib, I looked out of the kitchen window and saw the pit was as deep as a grave. The sky was clouding up. All I could see of the diggers was their ears. Then it got dark. The sun drops early in November. After it goes, you can maybe see the moon over the bay. That night there was no moon.

The next day after Ronnie went to work, I went out in the back yard to put clothes on the line. We have a washer Ronnie got second hand when the baby came. I do Laurette's wash every day. That day was one of those warm fall days when everything seems grey and brown. Smoke was everywhere—as though heavy clouds had come from the sky to rest on the ground.

I had the big bag of clothes pins tied around my waist. It felt as though I was expecting again. Heavy and lumpy. When the air moved, I saw the pit between the white diaper squares. The pit wasn't any shape at all any more—just wide. The inside looked dark and wet. I wondered if there were spiders in there.

Today is Sunday. Ronnie is resting. He works Saturdays. He rests Sundays. I am playing with the baby. She is trying to walk. She pulls herself up by the table and falls down again. We laugh about it. When she walks, I'll never let her go to the pit.

Last night, I asked Ronnie why the pit is getting so big. He is going to find out.

It's Monday now, Monday midnight. Ronnie will be home in a few minutes. Today I heard something about the pit from the girl next door. Her children are in school. She says she went down to the foot of the hill. She says the pit is coming this way. She says they are going to take the whole hill away. I don't believe her.

This is Tuesday. Last night in bed Ronnie told me something. He told me we might have to move. He heard it from someone at work. The pit is going to get bigger.

Wednesday. Today I didn't think about it, I didn't talk about it. Once, though, when I was changing the sheets on the bed, I saw something moving down there. It was a heap of rust-colored earth. It should have been standing still, but it wasn't.

Thursday now. This noon I cut my hand opening a can. Ronnie put a bandage on it. Before he did, blood ran down my arm. The baby cried at the sight of it. When the blood dried, it was the color of the red earth. If you try to take a handful of mud, you can't hold it. The more you tighten, the more it slips between your fingers.

Friday late. Last night I dreamed about the pit. Ron was snoring. I was sleeping with my head on his arm the way I always do. I woke up and couldn't go back to sleep. First in the dream the pit was somewhere inside of me, then everything reversed itself. I was lying down inside the pit and it fitted me like a glove.

Saturday. No one is working in the pit today, but the neighbors are talking about it. This morning I heard a man in the alley say they are going to take some of our houses away. I don't believe him.

I don't ask about the pit any more. I just keep the questions in my mind.

It has been raining for a long time. A cold rain. A brown rain. The afternoons seem like nights. There is twilight in the air—even early in the morning.

Last week, they took away the first block of houses. They waited until after Christmas. I don't know where the people who were living in the houses went. Somebody told me they are living in the pit. I don't believe it.

Did you ever watch water go down a drain that's almost clogged? Yesterday I was washing my hair in the shower, and the loose hair covered the drain in a ring. Do you know how you hate to touch something like that? It was my own hair, but I didn't want the dark ring in my hand. I got rid of it with toilet paper.

Another thing. I don't like cold weather and neither does Ronnie. The baby feels it too. Her little hands are red and chapped. Her bottom is sore.

Today a man came to the front door. Ronnie had gone to work. I didn't know whether to open or not. Finally I did. He said he was with the construction company. For a minute he stood there, looking at me with the baby. Then he said we wouldn't have to move. Not exactly. Our house was going to move, but we weren't. They were going to put our house and the others in the bottom of the pit.

What about the yard? I asked.

He said they couldn't move the yard. There wouldn't be a yard, but the house would be down there—safe and sound.

Then I thought about where would I hang the clothes or play with the baby when spring came. I thought about the sun. I began to cry.

Ronnie wants to do something about it. What can he do? Today he got up early. He went next door. He and the man next door went together down the hill. I think he went all the way down to the place where they are taking the houses away. I didn't watch where they went. Most of the time now, I keep the curtains closed in back. I don't want to look down that way any more.

Today it snowed. It snowed so much that you could forget where the houses had been. You couldn't forget the pit, but it got all soft and white. It could almost have been a pond or a valley or a natural thing. The men—I suppose they're hundreds now who work in the pit—didn't come. Of course, they left their machines there. The machines do most of the work. They have machines that dig. They have machines that knock things down. The machines stand up like skeletons against the snow.

Now that the snow has melted, things are worse. The pit is nearer. Most of the hill is gone. Most of the houses have been taken away.

The day the machines got to our house, the baby cried all day.

It's spring now, but you'd hardly know it. All we can see of it is a little piece of sky. Our house is in the same place as all the others. We are living in the bottom of the pit. Ronnie says we'll get used to it. I listen, but I don't hear him....

The baby is walking now. We've been living in the pit all summer. The hill is gone. All the houses are down here. It's cooler, Ronnie says. That's one good thing.

I haven't gotten used to the spiders though. There are spiders in the pit. Some of them are as big as my hand. They are hairy and dark.

Now it's November again like last year. It's safer in the pit, that's what everyone says. More people are living here. There's a store in the pit now.

I don't go out of the pit any more. It's a long way for me. I'm getting heavy. I don't know what has happened to the tracks and the bay and the city. I don't ask.

Today I heard something I didn't like. A lady told me there is going to be a *new* pit. Not a pit next to this one or somewhere else— a pit underneath. We won't be living in this pit any more, she says, they're going to move all of us down.

The new pit will be a lot deeper. The new pit will be safe.

I have been wondering whether we will be able to see the sky from the new pit. But I don't ask anyone, even Ronnie.

I think winter is ending, but maybe it isn't. Ronnie doesn't know. He doesn't go out to work any more. They have moved the plant down here. Everyone says it's a lot more convenient. No one minds. There are more stores now. There are theatres and restaurants. What else could you want? That's what people say.

Sometimes I think about the bay and the city, but I don't ask.

No one talks about them any more. Some people have even forgotten. I haven't. I remember how gulls circle. High and low, high and low.

Laurette is getting big. She likes to play with spiders. Ronnie says it's all right as long as they aren't the kind that bite. Most of those spiders are dead. I think they did something about them.

A lot more men wear brown clothes now. They are working in the new pit. Everyone has work, but there are children who don't know how the sun drops, how the moon rises. I'd like to see it all again, but the colors would be blinding. Even the moon would seem too bright. Ronnie is the same.

You don't see the new pit, but you feel it. It is underneath. There are rumblings when you sleep, tremors in the morning. When the house shakes, the spiders scurry faster. The baby laughs. She is beginning to talk.

"Spider." That was her first word.

Right now I am taking a shower. My stomach is big. I can hardly see the grey soapy water running down my legs as I wash. My skin is stiff. When the house started to shake, my stomach stopped moving. My stomach is like a stone.

There is something in the drain. It isn't hair curled like a crown. It's a spider with hairy legs. His legs radiate like dark rays of a dark sun.

The house is shaking. I hear Laurette laughing. I take the spider up in my hand. He curls in his legs. He is very still. He doesn't bite or jump. I let him sit in my navel. He likes that. He remains still.

I wait for him to spread his legs again. I look at his eyes. He looks at mine.

⊨ Plant ⊨

"...there is no single difference which separates all plants from all animals.... The inevitable conclusion is that plants and animals are very similar in many ways and that they have arisen in their development from common ancestors."

—Henry J. Fuller, *The Plant World*, New York, 1941

PERSON

When he is strong enough, he comes out in the morning to the back gardens, opens the hedge gate and makes his way across the broad, unmown fields to the high and distant bank overlooking the main road. There, below the old, scraggly pines, the side routes join in like branches meeting the trunk of a tree.

He is small, white-haired, shrunken. His eyes are clouded, his ears still sharp. The Home doesn't let him take a lawn chair way out there. When he gets tired watching the traffic passing, he sits on a flat, grey stone.

PLANT

In the dark, deep beneath the stone, in the dry dust flooded with exhaust fumes. A seed. One seed. Dessicated and small.

PERSON

When the spring rains come, he does not go out. He sits beside his window facing the sodden garden, the greening fields and the pines that look so dark from a distance. Behind the pines, the roads are hidden as if they did not exist.

He does not like to stay in his room with the white iron bed, the white blanket, the white iron radiator, the white-curtained window, the brown linoleum floor. After breakfast, he paces the hall: sun room at one end, dining room at the other. In between, brown wooden doors open into other white-curtained, brown-floored rooms.

Many of the people in the rooms do not walk. They sit. They lie. They listen to the rain. They sleep. Sometimes, they cry.

PLANT

Seed in the rain. Swelling, bursting. Weak and thin, the new stem pushes. Finds a way around pebbles, through worm trails, up. Towards the light, up.

PERSON

In early summer, he comes out almost every morning. From the back door of The Home, he follows the path of light. The gardens, the hedge, and then the fields recede. He arrives again at the same place, the flat stone facing the roads' meeting.

Below, at the bottom of the high bank, beyond the gravel shoulder of the highway, cars and trucks are going east, west, unknown destinations. They are going, he is not going. He is an old body watching from an old stone.

PLANT

Under the stone, out from under the stone. Expanding, ascending, meeting the light. One shoot.

PERSON

On a July morning of a soft-boiled egg and a chicken dinner to come, he arrives again at the rock. It is a slow, hot Sunday. Only a few cars, a few trucks. Long, empty stretches of grey asphalt.

The woman down the hall, Lila, the one who coughed so—she died last night. From light to darkness, the unimaginable journey.

Two red trucks in tandem. Then a motorcycle. Then nothing. Gravel left by the makers of the highway is scattered in the dust beside the stone amidst pale brown pine needles and white plastic cups thrown from cars. Also, on the sunny side of the stone, there is something new. It is a green shoot rising from brown dust, possibly a weed.

Church bells. Noon. Time to go back. Dinner.

PLANT

Leaf, leaf. One leaf. Its veins lengthening, branching. One leaf turning to follow the sun, and roots stretching far for rain.

PERSON

They say The Home once belonged to a family. The family laid out the back gardens. Once, there were many flowers. Now, the flowers are few. They are the flowers of professional gardeners—not the flowers of a family. Many beds have only ivy, neatly trimmed.

The garden paths are brick. They are straight and meet at right angles. Along the back hedge, which is privet, there are plots where persons who live in The Home can plant. Almost no one does. The woman who died, Lila, did. She had snapdragons, petunias, poppies.

Who will tend them?

PLANT

Leaves, two leaves, branching out to sun on thin stems. Dry roots stretching, searching.

PERSON

Today he goes twice to the highway. After breakfast, after lunch.

They are painting the hall of The Home. The hall will be whiter than white. New paint smells in the heat. The heat is worsening— no rain for many days.

When it is hot, the cars glide by with closed windows. Occasionally, a truck with a window down, a relaxed elbow lolling. Once, an old blue roadster, top down. And leaning way out in back with tongue extended, a spaniel with long ears flying.

Once, he himself had a dog. No particular kind of dog. A white dog. The dog died. Before that, his two sisters died, and before them, his mother. The dog was the last to die.

Where do the dead go?

PLANT

Dry, dry. Roots writhing in dust, leaves turning down, sinking.

PERSON

Hot and hotter, but still he hikes to the highway. They are painting his room. It is good to be free of the smell.

Beside the stone. In the dust and scattered gravel, that plant is still there. The oval, red-veined leaves are limp. The light green pattern rising along the center vein is tipped with dry brown.

It is not a weed. It is too beautiful, too strange.

PLANT

One leaf fallen, one leaf hanging. Stem weakening, draining, draining. Roots thinner than worm ways. Dry. Drying to dust.

PERSON

That same day, he comes again after supper—to get away from the paint. Again, he rests on the grey rock. Stark against the sunset, the plant stands bending. A plant risen in car fumes from refuse and dust. It is not a weed. It is some other lovely thing. It is dying.

Could it live in Lila's garden? Why not? Try.
Love. Rescue.

PLANT

Stretched...stretched...severed. Roots sundered, writhing dryly
in light. In warm light...in cooler light...in no light....

PERSON

Back across the fields he hurries in twilight. Through the privet
and across the bricks to Lila's earth. No trowel. No hoe. But there
in the privet, an old, earth-darkened fork—perhaps hers. There is
room behind the snapdragons, a place for a hole. He digs it.

PLANT

New earth, new air. But dry, dry.

PERSON

Unseen in the darkness, he goes in, takes the bedroom pitcher,
comes out. Poured once, taken in, filled again. Poured.
Earth patted, hands muddy.
Late to bed. Both of us.

PLANT

Rain with the first light. Rain and more rain. New air, new
water. Roots expanding, stems straightening.

PERSON

On the rainy morning, he puts on his old green jacket. He visits
the plant. The plant is not dead. The plant will live.
That day he asks for, and is given, Lila's garden. He will tend
her snapdragons, petunias, poppies. He will tend the plant from

beside the stone. That plant is his, his only.

It rains every day. He goes out every day. His green jacket gets wet. Within the wet green jacket, his heart is sometimes pounding. He does not have the white dog or the others who died before, he has plant, and plant has new leaves.

Each leaf is the same, each leaf is different. Oval, rising alone on a papery stalk, each leaf is divided by a straight, red-purple vein. From this conduit rise smaller, upward-curving veins. Each vein grows opposite its brother, each vein shares the blood of all.

PLANT

Light. Rising to light. One new leaf unfolding. Then another. Another.

PERSON

Because of his cold, he has not been to his garden. It has been raining, but today it is not raining. He leaves his bed. He puts on his clothes. He puts on his old green jacket. It is an effort. Because of the rain, he does not need to bring the pitcher. That is good. The pitcher is heavy.

Slowly out to the garden, slowly over the bricks. The long, soft morning shadow extends to greet him. The plant has risen. The plant is taller than the snapdragons. The plant's new leaves are turning, all turning, outstretched, palms to the sun.

A welcome.

PLANT

Branching, spreading. And soon, a flower.

PERSON

His fever is over, but he coughs in the early fall mornings. With the waning of summer, the sun is later in its risings. In his garden, he has discovered the plant's tiny flowers.

Each flower is lavender, streaked with white. Four fingernail-thin petals point in four directions. Four flesh-pale stamens, yellow pollen at the tips.

Shrinking to the size of a bee, a moth, he would spend the last of the warm days *there*—in the hidden shadows where the stamens join.

PLANT

Flowers closing in cooler nights. Petals shrinking in waning sun. Seeds to the winds.

PERSON

It is raining again. Long, chill fall rains. Coughing, coughing, he still goes out in the mornings. Someone has given him a camp stool. When it is not raining, he sits.

Buttoned tight in his old green jacket, he watches the oval, red-veined leaves. They move. In the morning, before the sun reaches their part of the garden, the leaves stand almost straight up. Well before noon, on a warmish day, they have spread and flattened, palms, as it were, always angled to the light.

After supper in the early twilight, if he feels strong enough to come out once more, he finds the leaves have again risen. Folding, rising, they are shut in on themselves.

PLANT

In the light, over and over, the familiar shadow passes, lingers, returns. The warm, moving shadow never shades, never stands in the way of the light. When rain is lacking, water is brought. When soil is hard, it is loosened.

Cooler in the light, cooler in the darkness. Then, rain or sun, the shadow does not come.

PERSON

Coughing, coughing. He measures time by the coughs—like a ticking clock.

They tell him that he cannot go out, will not go out, should not go out. In the freshly painted white room with the white bed, the white radiator hisses in warning: "Ssssss...ssssss...."

Despite the warnings, there is a Sunday after supper when no one is noticing. Coughing, still coughing, he pulls the white blanket back. Old feet tremble their way into old slippers. Old slippers shuffle over brown linoleum. Instead of the old bathrobe, the old shirt and trousers and the old green jacket. No one passing in the hall. No one noticing. Twilight.

Tiptoeing out, his heart pounds for the visit, anticipating. He pushes the heavy door, pushes. He is out. The bricks of the path are cold through the slipper soles. Slow, slow over the path's turnings.

And there, *there*, higher than the snapdragons, silhouetted against the hedge, underlining the yellow-grey sky from which the sun has dropped to the other side of the world, is not one plant but a clump, a profusion, almost a forest of plant brothers.

In the cool, clean wind of the coming winter, the plants are moving, welcoming the old man in the old shirt, the old trousers, the old green jacket, the old, thin slippers. Oh the leaves swaying, the last of the small lavender flowers swaying, and the stems, the many stems, strumming in the wind, strumming.

Oh the plants' song! Oh the soft, sweet humming! The roots add their long, slow heartbeats. His old legs sway to the music—the muted chorus of fall, the measured cadence of the passing of summer, the elegaic melody of cooling nights and shortening days.

And then his legs, no longer trembling, are gently, contentedly resting on the bricks. On the earth his head is pillowed. On the soil he tilled and tended are his old, thin arms extended. Sweet, clean breaths of moist, cool soil. The oval leaves, spotted and red-veined with their strange, centered patterns of irregular, light green streams rising against dark green are above him, swaying, caressing. Beyond the leaves, rising, rising is the yellow harvest moon.

Curling and bending, the leaves soothe his old cheeks; warm his fever-chilled forehead. It is good to be out of the white room, overshadowed, protected. He breathes slowly. He does not bother to cough. And then, relaxing, drifting toward sleeping, he does not bother (why now bother?) to breathe but once, then once again, then not at all—oh night, oh still and darkening night.

PLANTS

Bending, we are bending to cover the fallen shadow with falling leaves, with loosening petals, with sinking stems. Our roots are drying, drowsing.

The first frost. The night of declining, shrinking, dying. Old leaves cover old flesh, but the seeds, the seeds of spring are scattered, scattered far and wide.

⊸ Daddy Cerements ⊸

"The Great Chief, Death.... One side of him was beautiful; but the other side was rotten, maggots dropping to the ground."

> *The Hero with a Thousand Faces*, Joseph Campbell, Bollingen Series XVII, Princeton University Press, 1949.

"...he shall restore the world,...never grow old and never die, never decaying and never rotting...master of his wish...."

> "The Zend-Yasts," *Sacred Books of the East*, F.M. Muller, editor, Oxford, Clarendon, 1883.

"Oh do not mourn for me.... Oh, do not mourn.... Oh do... do *mourn...."*

That is the querulous, irresistible, slime-in-the throat voice of DC—Daddy Cerements.

Sometimes he appears in my room, materializes in my garden, or lies, covered with a thousand slugs, in my bed....

I am Monica, orphaned as an infant, raised by kind strangers. They died. Having attained the age of majority, I live on in their house. I am a student. Early one morning, going down the long hall to the back room, I discover my incubus.

I am looking for a picture of my dear adoptive parents. One was taken in some gardens on their final trip abroad.

The storeroom door is half-open. Inside, on a great green pall of a bed I have never seen before, Daddy Cerements lies mouldering. At first, I cannot see him clearly. The sun from the window by the bier is blinding. Also, in what is left of his left hand, he holds a little mirror—casting knives of light.

I smell him. I hear his obscene, compelling voice: "Come, *come*."

I freeze. What has happened to my parents' books, papers, mementoes? Where is his framed diploma, her wedding dress?

Instead of denying the nightmare, slamming the door on what cannot be, I stay, I stare. Shielding my eyes against the brightness, I see his bones poking through his fingertips like dry sticks, his elbows protruding like stumps from missing patches of flesh. His nostrils are non-existent, his eyes lidless. His hips rise like bare craigs from the soft, ragged, brown robe he wears half-open—loosely gathered by a stained sash.

"Come," he repeats, "*do* come—" He drops the little mirror amidst the rags of his satin coverlet.

I advance. Each step I take seems enormous, but it is tiny. It is half my lifetime before I reach the bed. Present to past—I can't resist. I take the proffered hand.

His odor overwhelms me like anesthetic. His half-fleshed hand rises to my wrist, then to my shoulder, then down. Soon, I am lying beside him, cushioned by fragments of his flesh.

What could be more repellent, impossible, irresistible?

Later, we drink tea together from the table beside his bed. In the background I hear—perhaps coming from an old-fashioned music box I cannot locate—the tinkling notes of a familiar but unidentifiable melody....

Daddy Cerements has become an occupant of my house: he comes and goes as he wishes. I can continue to attend my classes, but I can't be sure I'll be alone when I return. Perhaps I am never alone. His touch chills my flesh. His smell stifles my breath.

Time passes. My life has become impossible. I am planning my escape.

To leave will mean giving up everything. I will have to go to a strange place where I know no one, have nothing.

My plans are complete. I have kept silent. I am certain Daddy Cerements does not suspect. Our relationship continues as before. When he materializes, I greet him ardently.

The last evening—I will leave before morning—it is difficult to conceal my joy. When he questions me, I am silent.

I have decided not to travel by land, leaving tracks. Instead, I travel by water. On the steamer, I stand on the back deck, watching the waves of the wake opening outward. The pattern reminds me of DC's extended arms. How far is his reach? The salt smell is not as strong as his odor remembered.

When I reach my destination, a remote peninsula, I book a room in an old waterfront hotel. In the chill days of fall, I walk the beach alone. Waves erase my footprints; mind retains his image. Daddy Cerements—a wave rises. Daddy Cerements—it crashes and retreats. *Daddy Cerements....*

I rent an apartment by the month in a three-storey wooden building. Mine is the top apartment on the north. Like the others, it faces the sea. It is off season, I am the only occupant of the building.

I live there alone, quietly, without conflict. I join the public library, continue my studies. Sometimes I sit at my window for hours facing the sea. I am between lives. My life with Daddy Cerements has ended—hasn't it?

Winter comes. The little public square at the end of the board-walk is almost deserted. The fountains have been turned off. Most of the shops have closed. Often when I walk the beach, I meet no one.

Then, a few days after Christmas, I begin to hear little noises— the muted clanging of a plumbing pipe, a faint scratching on a distant wall. One icy morning, I hear someone singing. I am paralyzed. The voice seems familiar. Have I been discovered at last?

After breakfast, tiptoeing down the stairs for my morning walk, I hear music coming from the second floor apartment on the south side. Looking up from the beach, I see a curtain pushed aside, and deep within, a light.

I stay away from my apartment for the rest of the day, eat dinner in a restaurant, and afterwards, see a film. When I finally have to go back, the second floor apartment is blazing with lights. Daddy Cerements, I recall, often stays up late.

I unlock the back door of the building very quietly, climb the stairs on tiptoe. Nevertheless, just as I am stealing by, the door of the apartment opens. I do not see the one I expect and fear. Instead, it is a small, pudgy, pink-faced man carrying a bulging white plastic sack of garbage. Within, silhouetted in a rectangle of light, is a tall, angular woman with dark hair.

"Good evening." He greets me formally in a rasping foreign accent.

I nod, smile, and without speaking, make my way upstairs as quickly as possible.

Later, when I have bolted the door and switched off all the lights, I wonder whether I have ever seen the man—or the woman—before.

Since we are the only ones living in the building, we are bound to become acquainted. I meet the small man and the tall woman on the stairs, at the garbage cans, strolling the beach.

Their name is Ermholtz, I learn that much, but there is no explanation of where they are from or why they are living at the beach in winter. Why pry? They are old enough to be my parents.

Winter drags on. There is something about Mr. and Mrs. Ermholtz I do not like. Is it that they are physically ill-assorted, aging, unattractive? No. It is their grating accent, their fawning manners, their obsequious courtesies.

Our "friendship" begins with the predictible exchange of greetings, and then, small gifts. The first is a pale, circular sugar cake with a glazed cherry in the center. The cake is wrapped in white paper, tied with red string, and placed, ever so neatly, on top of my morning newspaper outside my door.

The gift is so formal and its flavor so delicate (almond? anise?) I decide to pen a note of thanks. When I am sure they are not at home. I slide my envelope under the Ermholtzes' door.

Not long after, there is a note of response to my note. Accompanying it is a white linen handkerchief embroidered with my initials. What am I supposed to do with it—cry?

My suspicions that they are emissaries sent by DC to search me out may be groundless, but I cannot escape their effusive attentions. When I pile discarded newspapers outside my door at night preparatory to carrying them to the garbage cans in the morning, they are spirited away. Later, I discover them neatly bound with twine resting on top of a new green garbage can painted "ERMHOLTZ" in white, slanting letters. The can, I notice, has an unusually unpleasant odor.

Later, I wonder how they noticed my papers from the floor below. How often have the Ermholtzes mounted the carpeted stair to my floor and stood silently in my hall—or even, at my door?

The door is not particularly thick or sturdy. The next day, I notice that two small eye holes have been drilled through the door at waist level. The holes, as I examine them, appear very old. It does not seem possible that.... I plan to plug them up, but forget. Instead, I puzzle for a way to repay their small courtesies.

Despite their attentiveness, the Ermholtzes have never invited me into their apartment. Although I notice, passing in the hall, its sweet, artificial smell, I have no knowledge of their taste. A small, decorative gift seems impossible. Yet my finances are limited; it would tax my resources to take them for a meal at one of the few seaside restaurants open all winter.

The next day, returning from a cold walk on the beach, I catch sight of the couple standing at their front picture window. Like costumed automatons, they wave in unison. It is impossibe to ignore them, I wave back.

An idea of how to repay them occurs to me. On a side street off the village square is the Candlelight Tea Room, a remnant of the days before motels and ramshackle wooden apartment buildings. I decide to invite them for afternoon tea.

The following morning, I proffer my suggestion, and it is immediately, avidly, accepted. We agree on the following Wednesday at three.

The day of the tea party it rains heavily—a white, solid, slanting flow that is almost snow. After breakfast, the Ermholtzes call, offer to drive. I accept. I will meet them at 2:45 p.m. at their car.

The time comes. Despite the weather, they are dressed up. He wears a fine, grey suede jacket with ribbed bands of wool at neck and wrists. She wears a flaring, fitted, old-fashioned rose wool coat. The inside of their car smells as if something had been burned in it. Neither of them smokes.

The rain is so violent that the streets are almost empty. Grey, icy water is rising in the gutters. We are able to park in front of the tea room, but in order to get out, I have to leap a rush of water. By the time we are inside, Mr. Ermholtz's grey jacket has been blackened by rain, and Mrs. Ermholtz's rose-colored coat has become a painful red. Finding a table is easy, we are the only customers.

I have never been in the tea room before—only peered through the lace-curtained windows. The seating consists of three-legged metal chairs and worn, pale pink plastic banquettes flanking the walls. The tables are round, black-topped, shiny. The narrow, overly warm room is lined with spotted, wall-mounted mirrors that reflect each other confusingly. The light of grimy wall sconces with crooked shades and an ancient chandelier with flame-shaped bulbs does not disperse the shadows. The rug is the color of dust.

The Ermholtzes take a banquette, huddling side by side like crows on a branch. Perched on a rickety chair, I face them—and a wall of mirrors. In such an anachronistic place, I half expect to be served by an aging waitress in a black silk uniform with white, starched collar, cuffs and apron. Instead, the server is a broad-chested, black-bearded man in a none-too-clean cook's jacket and puffy hat. There is a large, reddish-purple birthmark on the side of his neck.

Oddly, he smells of fish.

"Order when ready," the waiter instructs us brusquely, placing a wire stand containing a grey card of printed selections between us.

I give the card to the Ermholtzes to examine, then scan it myself. They choose *cafe au lait*, I order blackberry tea. We are promised our choice of a tray of pastries. The coffee and tea come promptly, accompanied by waxy, deckled-edged paper napkins. While we wait for the pastries, polite conversation is attempted: the intransigence of the weather, the hope of spring.

"Where we used to live," Mrs. Ermholtz volunteers shyly, apropos of nothing, "we often went to concerts...."

Is she talking about New York, Chicago, possibly the coast? She does not identify. Conversely, I imagine the couple at an old-time European spa.

By the time the pastries arrive on a finger-marked glass serving plate, my tea is cold. On a crumb-strewn lace paper doily, thickly frosted confections stand in rows like tombstones. The Ermholtzes choose Napoleons. I select the one chocolate eclair.

"We took long walks in the formal gardens...." Mrs. Ermholtz continues dreamily, as if talking to herself.

Is the pastry of my eclair unusually heavy or merely stale? I am unable to pierce the crust with my fork, I have to ask the waiter for a knife.

Mrs. Ermholtz consumes the layers of her Napoleon from the top down. First she eats white frosting scarred with chocolate crosses, then the first slathering of pus-colored custard. Mr. Ermholtz's plate is empty. He has wolfed his confection, almost in a single bite. Then, as if he had been talking from the beginning, he continues his wife's recollections.

"The garden paths circled the bandstand," he informs me. "It was a maze, but the music was always there behind the high hedges, leading you back, preventing you from being lost."

I am not listening. I have succeeded in separating a chocolate-engulfed morsel from the cement-like eclair. Hungrily, I raise it to my lips.

"If you become confused on the inner path near the fountain of the fauns...." Mr. Ermholtz drones pedantically, as if giving difficult directions, or perhaps, a warning.

Chewing my first bite is harder than cutting it. I have to grind my jaws together, and as I do so, something that does not seem to be custard slides down my throat. I cough.

What *is* Mr. Ermholtz describing? I am lost among his fountains and allees—yet at the same time preoccupied with the two, silky white hairs that protrude from the left side of his nose, swaying as he talks. Now that Mrs. Ermholtz has stripped the rubbery layers of her Napoleon down to her rosebud-patterned plate, she is *humming.* Above her head a flame-shaped bulb flickers—as if in accompaniment.

I try to swallow, fail. What *is* it that the eclair—so heavily coated with oozing chocolate as to conceal its substance—contains?

"—and beside the swan pond, a delightful carousel—" Mr. Ermholtz's remarks seem to be coming from a great distance. Mrs. Ermholtz's humming is louder. Surely, the tune is familiar.

I eject what is in my mouth into the too-small tea napkin, then, seeing no place to deposit it, hold the warm, unpleasant bundle in my hand.

I am unwell. There is an exceedingly odd taste in the back of my throat. I am beginning to feel dizzy. Food poisoning? Dangerously infected custard?

The waiter has disappeared. Yet, reflected from a hidden corner, I see his birthmark flash crimson. Something is fishy. I smell disaster.

The flame-shaped bulb has stopped flickering. Instead, the entire chandelier is revolving slowly. The table turns to the humming, in time with that music box melody. In the ancient mirror behind their heads, I see the Ermholtzes' faces reflected from across the room—doubled, redoubled.

Somehow, the Ermholtzes have possessed themselves of both my hands. "We are your *parents,* your *true* parents," they tell me in exultant voices. "We will not be dead."

My hands are crushed and kneaded between theirs. I am hard-pressed to keep the spit-out custard in the thin napkin from flowing between my fingers into theirs.

The leaden chocolate covering is sliding from the remains of my eclair into my plate, revealing a putrid confection covered with blue spots of mould. Just before I lean towards it and begin to retch, I see in the mirrors that the Ermholtzes now look remarkably alike. They are, in fact, the same person. They are—not a person at all. They are—I should have known from the beginning—Daddy Cerements. My eclair is not made of custard—it is his flesh.

Once you know a situation is unavoidable, you almost cease to mind it. I know now I will always live with Daddy Cerements. Like memory, he is inescapable. Daddy and Mommy Ermholtz were only one of his disguises. He has others, many.

I have grown used to him. I barely mind the smell. I am back in my house. I am continuing my studies. What is upsetting is when DC comes—as he does now more and more—in the guise of a young man, about my age, with golden hair.

Yesterday, the young man reappeared. When he wanted to kiss me, I drew away. But if he returns, perhaps....

⤚ I Told You So ⤙

"Don't talk to me, Mildred, I'm busy."

"I don't want to talk to you, Caroline. Please pass the scissors."

"I'm *using* the scissors, and please don't call me Caroline. My middle name is Lucy. That's what Father always called me."

"Mother called you Caroline. It was *her* name, after all. If I can't have the scissors, I won't be able to fix the rip in the veil."

"Take them, Mildred."

"You don't have to be snippy about it. It was you who tore Mother's veil to begin with."

"That was almost forty years ago. No one but you remembers— or cares. It wasn't anything I *did*, you know; it was a loose nail at the end of one of the pews. If you can remember a thing like that, you can remember to call me Lucy."

"I'm through with the scissors. Maybe you were in too much of a hurry coming down the aisle."

"All brides were in a hurry in those days, you know that."

"There's no reason for me to know about brides—never having been one."

"Sometimes I scarcely feel I was one myself—with him getting killed that same year in Korea. We had two weeks before he left, and that was all. No wonder I was in a hurry. Today it's all changed. It's five years, no, more than that—it was after Mother died—that Rory's had her living in his apartment."

"Caroline—"

"I won't answer to that."

"Caroline-Lucy-Morton-Renfrew—"

"You're acting childish. See how neatly I've stitched the veil to this little band I bought that will keep it on her head. Amanda is lucky. It's not every bride these days who has a veil of Rosepoint lace."

"Rory is your son. He has the right to get married however he pleases, but I don't see the point of it. Why go to the trouble of a long white dress and a lace veil when you're as good as married anyway?"

"That's their business, Mildred, not ours. Now let's hang the veil in Mother's closet. Sex is a part of modern life, Mildred, we have to accept that. Couples aren't in a hurry to leave their own weddings any more—"

"Mother's trunk would be better—no dust. Besides, the cat might—"

"All right. We'll put it back where it was. Help me fold it so it doesn't get wrinkled."

"It's a good thing she's a tall girl. It's as long as a shroud."

"What a thing to say!"

"Well, if weddings now are only catch-ups on what's already happened, funerals aren't. Can't gild that lily."

"Don't talk like that—"

"You never listen to me. Father didn't either."

"That's not so. Unlock the trunk. Father *always* listened."

"It is unlocked. He listened to you. You were the smart one. I was like Mother. He didn't listen to either one of us."

"Just because I learned bookkeeping—don't leave me holding this veil, Mildred."

"I can't do numbers, but sometimes I see how things will happen. When they do though, I'm not supposed to say: 'I told you so.' "

"Well Mildred, I told *you* that the veil would look as good as new after we fixed it, and it does. I'm going to lock the trunk again. Come April, it will be all ready and waiting."

Dearest:
I am going to write this year the way I always have: because it's

your birthday. I get older every year, but you don't. You're just a boy.
Your faithful,
Mildred

"Please pass the pickles, Mildred—and finish your dinner. You've hardly eaten half of what's on your plate."

"I've been thinking...."

"About *what*, for heaven's sake? Pass the rolls too, while you're at it. That sewing made me hungry."

"About the veil and how you can see things through it, but not exactly. I know I've lived all my life in the same old house in the same little town. People think I'm simple, but sometimes—"

"Whoever said *that*?"

"Mother didn't, but Father did—once."

"I don't believe it. He was a kind man, a good man. Surely you remember that."

"It was the day after your wedding. You weren't here. I was only eighteen then, but I had a good figure."

"Yes, and blonde hair. I always envied that."

"When there's a wedding, it puts you in mind for something else to happen. Jamie Forest came to ask for me, but Father said I shouldn't because—"

"Jamie Forest? I don't even remember him."

"Well he wasn't anything like your Royal—an army officer and all that. He was just a farm boy. He was quiet, and maybe—simple as me."

"What happened to him?"

"He died."

"When?"

"The day after."

"*How?*"

"It was an accident with his father's shotgun. He was hunting with his brother out in the hills. The gun misfired."

"And all these years we've lived together in this house and you never told me?"

"What was there to tell?"

Jamie,

It isn't your birthday, but this can't wait till next year.

Why'd I have to let on to Caroline about you? What if she found these letters?

She'd think I was getting the way Mother got.

Your sweetheart,
Mildred

"The wedding's tomorrow."

"Don't remind me, Mildred. I don't know how we'll ever be ready. Peel the eggs and put the shells in the sink."

"You didn't have to give them their reception here. It's not that big of a house."

"Mother and Father always did things at home—weddings, funerals. Why shouldn't Rory and Amanda enjoy the house now? It'll be theirs eventually."

"When we go—"

"Yes. Now squash out the yolks in this bowl and devil them."

"I want to go first, but I don't know how."

"Don't talk nonsense. You don't have to learn *how* to die. Besides, I'm older."

"Only by two years."

"I'm going to put a speck of red pimento in the center of each half. That's the way Father liked them. You can arrange them on Mother's sterling silver platter."

"Plated."

"The wedding cake."

"I haven't forgotten, Mildred."

"Let me be the one to take it into the diningroom."

"There're a lot of people in there—"

"You come behind me. You can hold the swinging door."

"She was a beautiful bride, Mildred."

"She didn't tear the veil."

"Of course not—look *out!*—"

"Oh *dear*—"

"It's all right. The frosting's only smeared a little on one side. If we put that side toward the window, no one will even notice."

"How could I know Rory'd be coming through to get ice just when I was going the other way?"

"You couldn't, Mildred, but you should have let me go first."

"Should of.... Caroline—*Lucy*—did you see the way his face looked?"

"His face?—"

"Don't you remember how it was with Father—that week after he'd had the stroke before he was taken? There was one side of his face that looked the way it always had. Then there was the other side that didn't look like him at all. It was all drooped down and distant as if there was something covering it and—"

"Mildred—to bring that up at a time like this. They're going to cut the cake—"

Jamie:
You're the only one I have to tell this to.
If I tell her, she won't believe me.
I saw what was behind the veiled part of Rory's face. It was you-know-what.

Love,
Mildred

"Keep to the path, Mildred."

"My feet are going straight, but the path isn't. I'm following the coffin."

"There ought to be an easier way to get to our plot. Father liked the view from this hill. That's why he picked it. It's a good tick from the road."

"Tick, tick. Tick tock."

"Sssh."

"Is this what Rory wanted—to be buried behind Father and Mother?"

"I don't know. If any of us had ever known he had something wrong with his heart, we would have asked him."

"*Blue.*"

"Keep your voice down, Mildred. People are looking at you."

"Blue—I'm whispering. That's the spot I want—where the little blue flowers are on the slope behind Mother's stone."

"*Sssh.* The minister's beginning the prayer."

Jamie my own:
Let's get married.
I'm tired of this old lady body. I know where I want it put.
Let me know.

Mildred

"Why did I have to go and do that, Mildred? It seems I can't do anything right since Rory went."

"Don't take on. It's nothing but an old cup. It slipped out of your hand."

"It was Mother's."

"It didn't smash to smithereens. There're only four pieces beside the handle. I think I can mend it."

"It won't be the same."

"Nothing ever is. What do you think Amanda is going to do?"

"She'll have to work—just the way I did. She told me she's applying for a teller's job at the bank."

"And the baby?"

"She can bring him here. I told her that. We have three bed-rooms. Mother and Father's room is big enough for both of them."

"Then, after one of us goes, the baby can have—"

"I've already thought of that."

Dear Mother:

If I can write to one dead person, I can write to another. I hope you are not surprised to hear from me. It's been fifteen years.

I suppose you know: Amanda and the baby have moved to our house.

Caroline broke your blue willow cup. Don't worry. I am going to mend it.

> Your second daughter,
> Mildred

"Amanda—"

"Yes, Aunt Lucy."

"Come out in the yard with me so we can think about where to put the baby's playpen when it gets warm again."

"I'm coming."

"The best place would be right here. You can see it from the window over the sink in the kitchen. Amanda, that isn't what I wanted to talk to you about. It's Mildred. I didn't want her to hear. I think she's getting—like Mother."

"Are you sure? She's so good with the baby. He loves her. She makes him laugh."

"Maybe so, Amanda, one child loves another. But she's been writing letters to *dead people!*"

"To—"

"Not to Rory, she hasn't gotten that bad yet. It's mostly to some boyfriend that died years ago. Now though, she's started writing to Mother."

"How do you know?"

"Yesterday she walked down to the village to get some glue to mend a cup I broke. While she was gone, it began to rain. I went up to her room to shut the window. I guess she'd gone out in a hurry: she'd left letters on her desk, and some of them had blown on the floor."

"What did the letters *say*, Aunt Lucy?"

"Some fool stuff. Talking about getting married to this dead boy. Talking about death. Saying there was some veil she saw—well...."

"Maybe she's lonely. Maybe we don't make enough of her. She's never had much of a life—just staying home and taking care of your parents, and now, little Rory. You always said she was simple, but—"

"It was *Father* who said that. Anyway, simple-minded is one thing, Amanda. Daft is another."

"I don't believe she is. She's just old and—"

"Amanda, when she came back with the glue, I couldn't help noticing she had something else in the bag."

"What?"

"Postage stamps. Writing crazy letters is harmless, I suppose, Amanda, but what if she should get it in her mind to put on her name and return address and *mail* them?"

Dear Father,
There is something I think you should know.
Caroline is spying on me.

Your loving daughter,
Mildred

"I've mended the teacup, Caroline."

"I've asked you not to call me that, Mildred. Try to remember, dear. *Please.*"

"Take the cup. It's yours."

"Thank you."

"You're welcome."

"Mildred, I've been thinking, and Amanda thinks so too. You don't get out enough. I take care of the business, the shopping, go to the library, play bridge, but most of the time you just—"

"I like being with the baby. We enjoy each other. He's beginning to talk—"

"But Mildred, it's getting warmer. Amanda wants to come with us when we go to the cemetery on Memorial Day. I think it would be nice if we went over and had a picnic at the Battle Monument afterwards. They have picnic tables there, you know. You can see way down into the valley."

"I remember."

Dear Jamie:
> *They want me to come with them Memorial Day. I'm not going.*
> *I need to think things through.*
>
> > *Your,*
> > *Mildred*

"Mildred, what will you do with yourself?"

"I have things to do."

"I can't imagine *what*. Mildred, you're giving me a headache. The baby will miss you. Amanda and I will miss you. It's a beautiful day too. You should get out—"

"I may go for a walk."

"Well, don't go too far. Remember the time you thought you were going to see Mother at the Home and you got lost in the woods instead?"

"Don't worry about me. Maybe the trouble is—I haven't gone far enough."

"If you can't talk to yourself, just going along the empty street to where the woods begin, who can you talk to? To the trees?

"A woman who worked for Mother talked to herself when she was ironing in the cellar. You could hear her through the kitchen floor. She told me: 'If you talk to yourself, you know you're talking to a sensible person.'

"Maybe I'm a sensible person. Maybe I'm the other kind. When you're old, people don't take on so much. When you're young, they expect....

"Old as I am, I still know a maple from an oak, a holly from a pine. I know to walk on soft needles since there's no path. I know not to stumble where those tree roots are.

"Sun doesn't come with you into the woods. Clouds come, but become shadows. In the woods, pines, oaks and others don't have their own names. They are nameless as clouds, as shadows....

"To get out of the woods, go to the light. The light goes to the street. The street goes home. I'm going home. At home, everyone has a name.

"How would it be, Jamie, if Caroline were to get a letter from someone?"

"Amanda, come into the kitchen and shut the swinging door behind you—then I know she can't hear us."

"What is it, Aunt Lucy? You look terrible."

"The mail just came—and look—"

"What is it?"

"It's a letter addressed to me on Father's blue stationery. It almost looks like his handwriting—"

"Open it—what does it say?"

"It says—it doesn't say *anything*. It's just a piece of his stationery all folded up."

Dear Jamie,
I'm sorry about the other day.
I was going to walk into the woods. But I got tired.
                    Your,
                    Mildred

"Aunt Mildred, I have to talk to you."

"The baby's sleeping, Amanda. I just checked him."

"That's good, dear, and thank you—but please listen. Mildred, Aunt Lucy's upset. Aunt Mildred, why, *why* did you—"

"You're talking about the letter from Father."

"Yes, yes. At least you know you did it."

"Of course I know. I'm not crazy."

"Well if you're not, why did you do it? Don't you see what could happen? She thinks you're getting like your mother. She thinks she might have to send you—somewhere."

"No chance. They closed the place where Mother died. Said they didn't need it. Now people who are like that are out in the street on pills. They live in group homes, if they have homes."

"Well, Mildred, this is your home, and you and Aunt Lucy have been very good to take me and the baby in, so please, please don't mail any more letters."

"The baby's crying."

"Amanda, I want you to do this for me. She knows my hand-writing, but you can disguise yours."

"I don't think this is such a good idea, Aunt Lucy. I'm afraid that—"

"Amanda, I've taken care of Mildred ever since Father died. Who else was there to do it? Without me, she'd be—well, I hate to think where she'd be. She's never been quite like other people. She can read and write, she can sew and cook, and she's wonderful with children, but that's never been enough for her. She wants us to think she's empowered to do what others can't. So she's taken to 'seeing' things, writing letters. Imagine—using Father's blue stationery!"

"Sometimes people sense things, Aunt Lucy. Even before we were married, I can remember Rory's saying he might die young."

"Well, Mother had a brother whose heart went bad when he was younger than Rory. Intuitions are one thing, but letters are something else. I'm responsible for Mildred. I don't know what would happen to her if something happened to me. You'd have to—but don't let's worry about that. What I'm trying to say is, if I let her wander too far into fantasy, she may not come back."

"Maybe you're right."

"You'll write the letter then?"

"What do you want me to write?"

"Just this: 'Dearest Mildred, I cannot marry you.' What more can I say, Amanda?"

"Maybe we should put: 'Don't write any more letters.'"

"Yes, that's good."

"Shall I just sign it 'Jamie?'"

"Maybe you should put 'Love, Jamie.' Let's give her that."

"I got a letter today, Caroline. Caroline, did you hear me?"

"I don't answer to Caroline. Who was the letter from?"

"It was from Mother."

"Oh, *Mildred!*"

"She said I'd be getting a letter from Jamie. A good-bye letter."

"Yes?"

"She said not to believe the letter because Jamie didn't write it. She said, *Caroline, that you* wrote it."

"*Please*, Mildred—"

"You're crying. It's too hot here in the yard. I'm going to take the baby in for his nap."

Dearest Jamie:
    I'm not going to write any more.
    We'll be together soon enough.

                             Your own,
                             Mildred

Dear Mother,
    You understand everything.
    Don't worry.

                             M.

Dear Father:
    I want to settle this.
    Am I simple?

                             Your second daughter,
                             Mildred

"Where have you been, Mildred?"

"I told you I was going for a walk, Caroline. How's the baby?"

"He's fine—but that was right after lunch and now, it's almost four o'clock."

"I went to the post office, and then, because it was such a nice day, I walked all the way over to the place where Mother used to be. I didn't get lost, but nothing's the same. The building's all boarded up. There's grass a foot high in what used to be the gardens where we'd take her out for walks. You're crying again."

"I can't help it, Mildred. I can't *help* it. I got so worried about you. And those letters—oh, Mildred, those *letters*—"

"Excuse me for knocking. It's me, Mildred. Amanda wants me to ask you, are you well enough to come down for dinner, or do you want a tray? She's fixed something nice."

"I'm all right, Mildred. I just needed to lie down for a while."

"Is it all right if I open your door and come in?"

"Yes."

"Are you sick?"

"Mildred, you mailed more of those letters today, didn't you?"

"I did."

"I want to ask you please, *beg* you—don't write to them any more."

"And if I should *get* a letter from one of them?—"

"You won't. I promise you, Mildred, you *won't*."

"I *might*—"

"Don't talk like that. Mildred, it's not bad to imagine things, but you can't let those things take over. If you want to make up things, do it with little Rory. He likes stories."

"In a few years, he'll be in school—"

"Maybe by that time there'll be something else. If you like writing letters, maybe someone would pay you to do it. Or else, you could volunteer."

"Maybe, but I'm old. I never learned how to drive."

"So do something right around here. You walked a long way today. We're only two blocks from the village."

"Caroline, I mean, *Lucy,* I want to see the ones waiting on the other side, but I'm afraid of dying."

"Well so is everyone else who lives long enough to have time to think about it. I'm afraid too. Never mind. I'm getting up now. We'll go down to dinner together."

"Sister, I want to show you the letter I wrote this morning. No, don't look like that. It isn't like the others. I even bought new writing paper."

Dear Sir or Madam:
I am writing to offer my services as a worker. I can write letters. I can file alphabetically. I can answer the telephone. Please respond.
Mildred Morton (Miss)

"I sent out ten of them—just to places around here. The churches, the art center, the library, the funeral home—"

"Well, what did I tell you? That was a smart thing to do. I hope something comes of it. Maybe you'll get a job offer in a nice, white business envelope."

"Maybe, but I can't see it happening. If I ask you a question, Caroline, will you answer the truth?"

"Of course."

"Am I simple?"

"It's just a word, Mildred. It doesn't have to mean anything."

"It does though."

"Maybe you can put into a word what you want to be there—like filling up a not-full jar."

"I can see how that could be."

"Mildred, if you stitch the collar on his little shirt, I'll put the buttons on the pants. It's hard to believe Rory'll be two years old."

"Please pass the scissors."

"Here they are. Mildred, there's something I've been thinking about."

"What?"

"I made up my mind this morning. Mildred, I don't care if you call me Caroline."

"Are you sure?"

"It's the same as what I said about 'simple', isn't it? It's just a word."

"Maybe. I heard the front door. Amanda's home."

"Aunt Lucy, Aunt Mildred—"

"We're upstairs sewing, Amanda."

"There's a letter here."

"You see, Mildred, what did I tell you? Mildred, what are you staring out the window for?"

"End of summer days like this, clouds come and go so fast."

"Mildred?"

"Sometimes clouds stretch thin as veils, float miles and miles. You can see what's behind them—places you'll never go, possibilities that'll never happen, things with no names...."

"Mildred, if you're just going to stand there, I'm going down to get your letter."

"Ask Amanda, what color is the envelope?"

"Just a minute."

"Well?"

"Mildred, oh *Mildred*, she says it's blue."

"Are you honestly surprised it's not a job offer?"

"Well dear, I suppose I—"

"Hello Amanda, the baby's sleeping."

"Here's the letter. It's addressed to both of you."

"Caroline, don't you want to open our blue envelope?"

"Mildred, what are you doing?"

"I'm unlocking the trunk. You had your turn with the veil,

Caroline. So did you, Amanda. I'm not as tall as you two. When I put the veil over my head, it shrouds me all the way to the floor. You can see me, but not quite. I can see you, but not quite. There's a cloud of lace between us."

"Amanda, help me, we must get her to take it off."

"I'll take it off, Caroline Lucy, after you've opened our letter. First, say who you think it's from."

"The postmark's smudged, but it is on Father's blue stationery."

"But I didn't write it."

"Who did then?"

"*He* did."

"Mildred!"

"If you don't believe me, open it. See, *see!* I told you so! Am I simple? I'm throwing off the veil."

The Stone

Sometimes, strange things have to happen before good can follow. Those irregular things, which can come after a man like his own shadow, may take unexpected shapes. I know, because after my wife was run over, this happened to me, Michael Reeves, a thirty-five-year old certified public accountant.

The "shape" was nothing but a big stone in my own back yard; yet, six months after Phyllis had been killed by a hit-and-run driver, I began to allow that rock to direct my life.

It happened late one afternoon in January. I had come through the wooden gate to the high-fenced yard to clear a snow path to the back door. Unreasonably, I rested on the shovel, lingered by our biggest garden boulder. The day was sunless, the sky a putty-shadowed grey. With one gloved hand, I reached out, brushed snow from the unshaped rock.

The stone was the mindless color of mud. Its pox-marked surface had only a few redeeming tracings of rusty red, an insufficient scattering of mirror-mica flakes. Still, the shadow-weight of the thing drew me. Like a magnet, the boulder held me from my purpose.

I dropped the shovel, fell to my knees. Snow flowed against my closed eyes. When I opened them, blinked, the monolith was black against a glare of sky. I felt nothing but cold. I thought of nothing— nothing at all; yet I had become a convert.

What made this mysterious thing happen? Before I knew what the stone would ask of me or how I had been transformed, I troubled my memory, reexamined what lay behind.

The garden, of course, had been my wife's creation. We had honeymooned abroad; she had particularly wanted to see Stonehenge.

After that, we chanced on other ancient stone circles in Scotland and Ireland. The homey backyard remembrance she had made afterwards was nothing more than a ring of seven boulders caged from construction workers completing our development in raw fields. Six of the discarded stones were of modest height. The seventh was the singular monolith.

The next July, a year after the stones had been installed around a buried pail that served as a make-do pool, the accident happened. Phyllis had been doing some planting at the ring of stones in the cool of the evening. We usually jogged together after dinner, but I had a bad cold. So, at twilight, she went alone.

Just beyond our dead end street, she had been knocked to her knees, then crushed by a car that never stopped. The sole witness, a woman walking her dog, thought the car had been brown. She'd barely glimpsed the driver—couldn't give a full description. All she'd seen was white hair.

After Phyllis's burial, I was immobilized. First of all, I couldn't, *wouldn't* jog. To run in the development meant passing—virtually *stepping*—on the very place where she'd died.

Further, I refused to go to the garden. I let flowers wither; I failed to prune or pick. My excuse was that I'm red-haired, fair-skinned. The truth was that I loathed the fecundity of August. She was only twenty-eight; we had not even had time to have children. It was September before I picked up the trowel she had been using the night she died.

When it got cooler, I did come out one evening after work to sit in the wooden swing where we had often rested together. I was listless from lack of exercise—I'd tried jogging near my office after work, but the downtown rush hour traffic had been too much for me.

Somehow though, I had to rebuild my life. I had avoided my friends and my few, distant relatives since the funeral. What I wanted most—I kicked at the dirt beneath the swing and set it rocking— was to find the hit-and-run driver and confront, maybe kill, him.

The swing squeaked. I kicked the earth again, moved faster.

The sing-song squeaking was mockery. I had called the authorities only the day before. The case was still "under investigation," and, I suspected, might always be.

I jumped up. The swing's song followed. I could still hear it after I'd gone into the house.

That fall, I often ate dinner near my office, then went back and worked late. I was trying to build up the business. One night, driving home in the dark, I noticed a car parked in front of the empty lot at the beginning of our street. It was a brown coupe, and I caught a glimpse of someone with white hair sitting at the wheel.

I was tired. I had turned into our driveway—the last on the dead end—before the thought registered. Then, when I looked around, the car was gone, the street silent. There was no way to tell whether the brown coupe had turned toward the highway. All I could hear was a faint humming—possibly the swing squeaking in the wind.

It was almost November before I went to my yard again. Then, one Saturday afternoon, I set to work. First, I raked mounds of leaves that had fallen inside our grey board fence. I had started a regimen of daily exercises, but, out of fatigue or inertia, I often forgot. The physical effort felt good.

Slowly and painstakingly, I removed leaves from the ring of stones. There, I noticed how the monolith's shadow—stretching like an arrow or a sundial marker—blackened the leaf-clogged water in Phyllis's pool made from a pail. In that dark mirror, I saw my own shadow with the sun setting behind me. There was a cool breeze.

Even then, three months before my strange conversion, the big stone had made me uncomfortable. Beyond size, it seemed different from the others. Without having been carved as a statue or cut into a block for a building, it seemed to have *purpose*, even, *presence*.

It was getting late. My last job was to disassemble the swing for the winter. By the time I'd finished, the sky had turned smoke brown. After shutting the garden gate behind me, I started up the incline to the front yard with my leaf-loaded wheelbarrow. Then, cold and tired, I stopped short. There, at the end of the twilight block in the same place as before, was the brown car.

I was determined it would not escape me again. Dropping the barrow handles so quickly that loose leaves whirled around me in the rising wind, I ran as fast as I could. Light as a straw man, a creature of dust and hate, I raced to the end of the street where the driver— yes, he was a thin, almost emaciated man with white hair—had started his engine. I was not afraid, I waved my arms, the tails of my tattered work shirt flapped around me.

I did not care, I would not stop—but no—he was not going to run me over. Instead, seemingly startled, he put down his window.

"May I help you?" he asked a bit nervously.

"You killed her—" was what I wanted to shout. I wanted to reach for his throat. Then, taking stock of myself—I was covered with leaves and soil—I panted: "What are you doing here?"

"The post office's closed." He was eyeing me apprehensively. "I'm a composer after hours," he added quickly, "there's a sort of music coming from around here. I've come before to listen—but I never can find it."

"*Music?*" I blurted, trying to brush brambles from my chest. "*Post office?*" I had a thorn in my thumb. He was either brazen or crazy—I wasn't sure which.

He fingered the wheel apprehensively. I could see he wanted to go. Perhaps he thought I was crazy. "I'm writing a symphony," he explained. "What I keep hearing isn't a chord—it's more of a tone— it's—"

He could see I didn't understand. "I'm the postmaster," he added as an afterthought. "You know the place—up the road—"

"My wife died," I blurted. "She was run down over there—" I pointed with a wavering finger.

"Last summer?"

I nodded.

"I'm sorry—" He released the hand brake, "—very sorry."
The brown car began to move. "I think I read about it in the
paper—"

Like a grey figure in a grey dream, I was immobilized. I just
stood there, sweating. He would have stopped, of course, but I
didn't bar his way. I saw the license plate, but even as I committed
it to memory, I felt it wouldn't help me.

Slowly, I made my way back to the house, left the overflowing
barrow in the front yard. Let it ride, like the leaves, in the wind! I
went in, slammed the door behind me.

There, I stretched out on the rug like an angry child, hammered
my fists. For the first time since the funeral, I cried.

Later, to confirm what I believed to be the truth, I took the
opposite direction from my route to work, drove by the little rural
post office. Without going in, I glimpsed the white-haired composer
at the counter. In his uniform, he looked thinner than before—
almost insubstantial. His little brown coupe was parked neatly in the
gravel drive beside the building.

I turned around and did not go back. I always mailed my letters
in town.

Still, I wondered, could the postman's talk have concealed a
compulsion to return to the scene of the crime? After I'd learned
he'd had compositions performed, even written up in the paper, I
dismissed the possibility. Then, I had another idea. Had the "music"
he'd been seeking been only the ha-ha squeaking of the swing I'd
dismantled? If so, he wouldn't be back.

In December, flesh reasserted itself. For months, I had turned
down invitations from old friends, kindly acquaintances. Then, not
long before Christmas, a woman who had known my wife well called
me. There was to be a benefit dinner dance in town. She was selling
tickets. She had a friend, recently divorced, who....

The night of the party, I got out my best dark suit for the first time since my wife's funeral, imagined I could still smell the flowers flanking the altar, piled at the grave. When I got to the hall where the party was being held, I almost turned around. Then, as the double doors opened to admit someone else, I was drawn by the warmth, the brightness.

It was a big, rectangular, high-ceilinged place that doubled, at other times, as a gymnasium, a meeting hall, a setting for amateur theatricals. I had been there often in times past, but after my months of seclusion, it overwhelmed me. The strident music, the colored lights, the streamers suspended from the rafters were too much. I was about to turn away and go home when Phyllis's friend found me.

Seated at a table with convivial people, most of whom I knew, at least slightly, I soon got used to it. I took several drinks, relaxed.

The divorcee was attractive, even beautiful. Fortunately for me, the loudness of the music precluded conversation. I asked her to dance. Afterwards, we ate, then danced again for a long time. She was lonely, so was I. That she ended up coming home with me was not surprising. Nor was it surprising that, after a few weekends, the thing ended. Two raw wounds rubbed together do not heal.

At the beginning of January, the month of my conversion, I had an odd dream. In it, my wife and I were digging in our garden. She was shrouded in white. I was wearing my dark suit. The pail-for-a-pool was gone, and we were making a great hole in the place where it had been. As we dug, the soil became lighter, finer. At the bottom, we found white, gleaming sand. It was smooth and fine, almost golden.

When we stopped digging, the hole began to fill with sea-blue water. The water infiltrated, then softened the ground above. Then, as if on a mud slide, the six smaller stones toppled down into the pit one by one. After them came the monolith, making a great splash. All the stones sank out of sight, and the water remained fresh and warm and pure. So, casting our clothes aside, my wife and I lowered ourselves into what was fast becoming a beautiful pond.

There, we swam together for a long time, and as we circled, embraced, separated to circle again, we were singing, always singing a wordless and wonderful song.

It was several weeks after that when the conversion I have described took place. In the days that followed the afternoon I knelt in the snow, I expected something would happen. Instead, nothing. More snow fell, cold grey days faded into long, frozen nights.

It was tax season. To pay for Phyllis's funeral, I had taken on too many clients. Somehow, I took care of them. Day and night, I struggled with overdue payments, intricate returns, confusing records. My labors, though, were shadowed by another imperative. It was strong, but undefined.

What did the stone want of me?

Once, ostensibly to feed early-returning birds, I scattered an offering of bread crumbs around the enormous stone. The crumbs disappeared, but that was all.

Then, very late one night in March, my eyes glazed with exhaustion, I happened to glance down into the yard as I was getting ready for bed. There, gleaming in the dimness, was what seemed to be a ring of tiny white eggs around the monolith.

I was half-asleep, but I had to investigate. I went down to the garden in my bathrobe. When I got there, I realized I was barefoot, but I didn't go back. Making my way over moist earth, I reached the rock. Instead of eggs, I saw a ring of white crocuses was blooming in the half-light that preceded sunrise.

Amazed, I stood there shivering. I knew I hadn't planted the flowers. Had Phyllis—perhaps on the last night of her life?

As if to unearth an answer, I poked a toe into the soft soil between several plants. Then for no reason, avoiding the flowers, I began to circle the stone. My muscles were lax, winter-softened. The movement felt good. I began to sprint around the entire circle of seven.

In and out, round and round, faster—faster! Finally, I got dizzy.

There was rhythm to it, I had discovered, even a sort of music.

The next morning, I slept through my alarm, missed several appointments. When I got up, I didn't remember my excursion to the garden until I saw my muddy footprints on the kitchen floor.

What had I been doing?

I had no idea, but that day, in spite of being tired, I felt I had accomplished something.

Finally, the tax deadline came, the returns were finished. I was taking the next week off. After a day during which I slept most of the time, I set off to visit my wife's parents. Both were confined to the same nursing home in a small town on the other side of the mountains. Phyllis had made the trip monthly. I had not gone since the days following her funeral.

They were pathetically glad to see me. Each was more feeble than before. He had had a stroke that had left him unable to walk. She had been weakened by a series of heart attacks.

I spent the night nearby, visited them again the next day. When I said good-bye, both took my hands warmly.

"We want you to know," Phyllis's mother quavered, "that we *expect* you to marry again."

"Phyllis," her father insisted in the same kindly way, "would have wanted you to—"

I could—probably should—have spent another night there before driving back over the mountains. Still, I decided to make the trip. It was twilight, dark came almost immediately. The road was thin, curving, little-traveled.

At first, I was buoyed by the compassion of Phyllis's parents— then depressed. It was some time since I had called the authorities, I realized guiltily. Could—should—I have done more? As I drove through long stretches of dark woods between small, sleeping towns, my unfocused hate for the hit-and-run driver revived. Finally, I thought of the white-haired postman again. I had never even given his license plate number to the police. What if?—

I got home long after midnight—exhausted. Why hadn't I waited until morning? I wondered, still flailing myself. Then, as I got out of the car, I knew why I had driven so long, so late: *I wanted to see the stone again.*

Dropping my bag on the front walk, I headed for the garden gate. Inside, the ring of stones looked the same. I went to the monolith, knelt, finally touched it. The surface was a surprise. Instead of being rough and pox-marked, the surface was nearly smooth.

I stood up. In the light of a crescent moon, I saw a strange, glistening residue that had not been there before. It ringed the great rock like a wreath. Where bread crumbs had been, where crocuses had bloomed, where my feet had sunk into soft earth, was a sort of "sand." The stone, it appeared, was sowing itself in the ground.

When I returned to work, there was an urgent message waiting. The authorities had a lead in the case at last. When I called back, they said they'd be in touch again soon. The driver, I was told casually, had been a woman.

I was relieved, and at the same time, discomfitted. The idea of a woman—faceless, nameless—seemed preposterous. My long-harbored fantasies of violent confrontation with the postmaster, or possibly another man, faded, and I could not replace them. All I had left was pent-up anger—a dry cloud of choking dust.

The next day, I learned that no replacement was necessary. The woman driver was dead.

It was an odd story, told, a few hours later, by two policemen whose names I couldn't remember afterwards. On the evening my wife died, an old woman had gone to visit her daughter in one of the houses at the other end of the development. The woman was in her eighties, white-haired, hard of hearing. After dinner, she left to drive home to town. In the twilight, she felt a bump, heard nothing. Assuming it was a pothole, she drove on.

Later, the octogenarian noticed a dent in her car, told her daughter about it. She made an appointment to have it repaired, but she didn't keep it.

"Why *not?*" I'd demanded.

It was because, they told me, right after that, she'd had a stroke. Half-paralyzed, unable to talk, she'd lingered for months in a nursing home. The previous week—on one of the days when I was visiting Phyllis's parents—she had died. Soon after, the daughter had taken her mother's brown sedan to a garage. There, fragments of fabric, strands of hair were discovered and—

I'd barely listened to the rest of it. I *couldn't.*

The first thing I did when I got home was to call Phyllis's parents. Then—then I didn't know what to do with myself. After a few push-ups, I went to bed, fell asleep immediately.

It wasn't long, though, before I was wide awake. It was May, a warm night. The window facing the yard was wide open. There was a rhythm, a summoning.

I threw back the sheet. I didn't dress, I went to the garden in my undershorts. At the stone, I knelt. Pressing my ear to its smooth surface, I heard the strange humming—perhaps the echo of something far away. Like the sound of waves in a curved shell, the humming suggested, impelled activity. My previous, spontaneous circumambulations of the stone and its fellows, I saw, had not been enough. So, scrambling to my feet in an instant, I began.

Determined to out do myself, I raced across the garden, returned to the stone, leaped over it, circled the smaller stones, cavorted, danced, leaped, rose, almost flew. I was not going to stop, for, at last, I *knew* what the stone wanted. The stone, the great-but-diminishing master stone, wanted me to romp it to sand.

And my overweight, under-exercised body was gaining strength. I *could* do it. I *would* do it—I *was* doing it—I—

At the very moment that the garden gate opened wide, I was in the middle of an immense leap from the big stone to a smaller one. I didn't make it. Instead, I descended with both feet into the muddy water of the pool-made-from-a-pail.

The gate-opener, the unexpected and unwanted visitor was the composer—the postmaster in real life.

"I'm very sorry," he blurted. "I didn't think that you'd be—"

With what dignity I could muster, I extricated myself from the water. My feet were dark with mud, my legs mottled with wet leaves, my undershorts splashed, almost soaked, virtually transparent.

The postmaster was all in white. He was wearing a neatly-pressed white shirt (probably part of his uniform), well-tailored white trousers, and a loose white coat, unbuttoned, that flapped behind him in the breeze. His white hair waved around his pale, thin face.

Mud makes dissimulation difficult. Without explanation—but with a certain satisfaction—I blurted roughly: "I *suspected* you—"

He stared at me, drew back. "Of *what?*"

"Of killing my wife. You wouldn't know, but the car that crushed her was brown—and driven by a white-haired person. When you parked in your brown coupe I thought you were returning to the scene of your crime."

He grew even paler. "Of course I *didn't* know. I'm sorry—very sorry. I'm only the postmaster—I hadn't even been on this new street till last fall. I came then—just as tonight—for the music. Don't you *hear* it?"

"I *did* tonight," I admitted. "I do now." I returned to the monolith, stretched my arms around it as far as I could, impressed the dark shadow of my wetness on its surface. Then, sliding around so the stone stood between us, I said: "The driver was an old woman in a brown sedan. She's dead. I suppose I could still press charges—but—"

Amazed and silent, the postmaster stared at me.

"I wouldn't exactly call it music," I qualified abruptly. The breeze was cool. I was beginning to shiver.

"There's a *rhythm* to it," he insisted. "In the second movement of my symphony—"

"I'd say it's like waves breaking," I cut in, "like the beating of someone's heart."

I thought of Phyllis. She had been dead almost a year. "The music belongs to my wife's stone," I told him, not wanting him to have it for his symphony.

"Not just to the stone," he countered.

I didn't want to argue. Besides, how could I be sure? "Take it for your music if you have to," I told him reluctantly.

"I will." He smiled. I could see it made him very happy.

Everything about him seemed white, joyful. When the moon sailed out from under a cloud, he almost gleamed.

In contrast, I was muddy, dark as a shadow—except for my red hair. Although shivering miserably, I could not release my grip on the stone. Instead, pressing myself even more ardently against it in a strange embrace, I thought I saw that the great boulder was...like death...impersonal, mindless, cold beyond all imagining, blacker than a congress of all the nights. Even my forehead was pressed against the rock. The air I was breathing was musty, moist. It smelled like a grave.

Then, repulsion saved me. The stone was without life, so was Phyllis—but I *wasn't*. My heart hammered, my pulses pounded. I was strong. It was no effort at all to drop my arms, step back, emerge from behind the monolith and offer the composer my hand.

He gave me his. We shook in the aura of his expansive radiance, and the wind rose. The stone's "sand"—it was almost like a cloud of infinitessimal insects, a stream of air-borne seeds or a morning mist— floated around us. I was convinced I had done what the stone wanted, and I was glad. Whatever had to happen was over. Whatever would happen had begun.

All summer afterwards, as I replanted the garden, I watched the stone diminish. Unbelievably, when Phyllis's parents died within days of each other at the end of August, the monolith was the smallest of the seven. By November, when the garden had died down again, there was nothing but gleaming, grey-brown sand.

That winter, I joined a gym, took up squash, lost weight. Happily, that very summer, I married again. My new wife, Ruth, whom I'd hired a few months earlier to help with my expanding business, likes music. We also dance—but not in the garden.

Last year, not long before our first child was born, we attended a concert at which the postmaster's symphony was performed—and much praised. He conducted the work himself—wearing a black tuxedo and looking not-in-the-least emaciated. There was something in the second movement I thought I recognized—but I couldn't be sure.

This year, I got out the old swing again at the beginning of summer—then discarded it. Ruth didn't like the squeaking. Still, six of the stones stand in the garden where they were before. In the break in the ring where the monolith once towered, my little son plays with his pail and shovel. His sandbox is filled with glistening and unusual sand.

Dinner for the Dead

I didn't invite them, but I know they are coming. Who *would* plan a dinner party for the dead?

Furthermore, it isn't Halloween, All Souls, the Samhain of the Celts or even the end of October. It's April—a dark month of freezing rain and lingering ice promising only the hope of relief from a cruelly extended winter.

Some things can be controlled. Others, like the last, pitiless winds of March and after, can't. There is no way to send a message, beg off, say I'm not well, have been called away—anything. So, when the day comes, I get out the best lace tablecloth that I haven't used in years, take down my mother's Limoges plates from the top shelf of the china closet. As I fold the initialed napkins that were among my parents' wedding presents, my hands tremble.

The thought of seeing them all again—my parents, my husband, and *his* parents—isn't one I can easily picture. Will they look, I wonder, like themselves? A last, treasured photograph is one thing, but the actual presence is....

The one I want to see most, of course, is my father. He is the longest dead, the most loved. I lost him in childhood, but the pain has barely muted over the years. How much I have wanted, on innumerable occasions, to see him one more time! Now he is coming —but with the others—and that means I will have to hold back, be polite, deal with all the guests at once.

Sitting in my kitchen, polishing the flat silver, I think of my father's christening spoon, stolen years before along with other family pieces. Afraid, after that, of losing everything, I had put my mother's flat silver away in a safe place for my daughter. The set that the dead and I will be using is a substitute, even though it's sterling.

Odd, I muse as I work the pink polish between the tines of a fork someone has obviously used for egg, that only my mother and I have known all the guests, including the unwanted one, my husband's mother. There will have to be introductions, explanations. I will have to find out, tactfully, if the dead know what has happened in the lives of loved ones after their own passings. Does my father, for instance, know of my husband's early death, of my daughter?

Another worry is the menu. I have planned an old-fashioned meal —would they have invited themselves for dinner if they couldn't eat? Besides, I reason, if dead, one has no need to diet or fear rich and fattening foods. Traditional favorites seem the best choice.

When the time arrives, I have everything ready. Tall white candles rise from silver candlesticks; crystal goblets gleam. The table is set for six, but I am worried about seating. The table, a Chippendale piece my father bought long ago, is rectangular. This means one on each end, two on either side. I, the hostess, will sit at the end near the kitchen, the foot of the table. Who should sit at the other end, the head? Does seniority, i.e. age at death, or blood tie take precedence?

I am distracted, momentarily, by my grandmother's gilt-framed, floor-to-ceiling mirror hanging in the hall. Do I see a moving shadow —or only the reflection of the white, transparent curtains undulating in the chill draft from the slightly opened windows?

From which direction are the guests coming, I wonder uneasily —and from where? As if in answer, I hear the doorbell. Ten minutes early, but the dead have come.

I open the door.

The next minutes blur. I embrace them all, I weep. I cling longest to my father, then to my husband. I even peck the yellowish cheek of my mother-in-law, who tried to prevent her son from marrying, wanting to keep him home forever. But what is forever, I wonder, to the dead?

As we move from the hall to the dining room, I decide to place my husband at the head of the table even though he was the youngest at his death. Age, I see, does not affect the dead as it does the living. All of the five are entirely recognizable. They look as they did—yet seem neither young nor old. They embody a stasis I can't understand, a permanence I can't share.

I am enmeshed in change—swept hourly and inevitably toward death. The distinction between me and the others is vast, exhausting. In a way, I feel older than all of them.

Effortlessly, as if foredestined, the dead take their places at the table without my telling them. My husband is opposite me, my dear father is at my right, and my mother is next to him. My mother-in-law is at my husband's right, and beside her is my father-in-law, seated at my left.

After the blessing, my mother rises to help me serve big bowls of the thick, cream-colored soup I have made myself. Catching sight of her left hand with its familiar rings (one in the bank, I know nevertheless, the other in her grave) I am surprised she does not anger or upset me as she so often did.

In life, my mother had spoken frequently of doing good—but did harm anyway. In death, I sense, her good intentions have been realized. I love her.

Everyone eats my soup. The flavor is bland, but they seem to like it. In the chill, changeable, not-yet-spring weather, it fosters warmth and calm.

We chat as we eat, but the conversation is quiet, polite, inconsequential. There are so many things I want to tell my father, so many things I want to ask him. Half a lifetime of years and days lies between us, but I can't give them voice.

I begin to see that this dinner is not the sort of family reunion at which one "catches up" on what others have been doing. What, after all, *have* the dead been doing? And as to the lives of those who have lived on or come after—is it possible that?—

Everyone is finished, the gilt-edged china soup bowls are empty. Before I get up to clear, my father takes my hand. I remember his gentleness, his kindness to me as a child. He doesn't speak, but I understand. It isn't necessary for me to review the long years with-out him—he knows.

The next course is a standing rib roast of beef with Yorkshire Pudding, my husband's favorite. As I carry it in on the initialed silver platter, his eyes meet mine. I set it in front of him. He takes up the silver carving set as always.

The rest of the main course is equally traditional—oven-browned potatoes, carrots, onions. I ask my mother-in-law to serve them—I can see she is pleased. I pass the rolls. I pass the big bowl of brown gravy and the ladle. My husband slices the red flesh expertly, thinly with the long, silver-handled knife. He arranges neat slices on each plate, then passes it on to his mother for vegetables.

In death, I see, the intensity of the attachment between my husband and his mother is transmuted. Their closeness, which I had tried—and failed—to penetrate, has dissolved the way clouds shift, float aside and finally fade, leaving open sky.

I suspect that love—in its many forms—exists for the dead, but not in its individual aspects. Love for them is perhaps pervasive in a way I can sense—but not understand.

As we eat, I chat with my father-in-law, the doctor so devoted to his patients. I have to tell him of my daughter, the grandchild born after his death. He listens with what strikes me as professional patience as I describe her grace, her beauty, her many accomplish-ments. Talking on, I mention traits she may have inherited from him, interests they might have shared.

Although the doctor nods, makes appropriate comments, I sense that the intense interest I feel for my child—or would feel for a future grandchild, is not shared by the dead. When one is without blood, perhaps the ties of blood are diminished. Are the dead then "related" to everyone?

While I'm still talking, the doctor and the others clear their plates. For some reason, I'm not hungry. My father and mother are chatting jovially; my husband is engaged in a long, intense discussion, almost an argument, with his mother. Eventually, the doctor joins in.

The room is neither too warm nor too cold, but a damp draft is coming from somewhere. The stale, persistent flow makes the candles burn faster. As the flames rise, the still-uneaten food on my plate looks larger, heavier, darker. I circulate the tines of my fork in gravy, raise a lump of potato to my mouth. I chew, and then, add a piece of meat before I have swallowed.

Is it the musty air, the fading light? The food tastes like ashes in my mouth. I set down my fork. The dust-colored shadows of my guests expand. Blotches of darkness appear on the walls, down the hall. Something in the room is slightly noisome. I am unable to finish my meat and vegetables. Instead, I watch the elongated, slow-moving distortions of my upside down reflection in the bowl of the silver dessert spoon beside my plate.

The others are still talking, but my mother sees I am tired. The party is bleeding my strength. She begins to clear the plates, and dutifully, I rise to help her. I refill the water glasses, remove the roast—what's left of it—to the sideboard. Later, when there's more room in the kitchen, I'll strip meat from the bones.

As I set down the sundered flesh, my husband is standing beside me.

"I'll pour more wine," he tells me.

I nod, unable to answer. Why does watching him pour red wine into crystal glasses make me want to cry?

Awkwardly, I wait in the far corner of the room until he has finished. "I've needed you—" I blurt as he approaches with red stains on his hands, "so many times."

Between us lie memories of quarrels and misunderstandings. If he had lived, I've told myself many times since his unexpected passing, we would have learned to love more, argue less.

No one seems to be watching. For an instant, he takes me in his arms. "Forgive me—" I beg.

"Forgive," he echoes, "forgive...."

We separate, stand facing each other. "I'll come for you," he promises.

"I've known that," I tell him, "for a long time." When he returns, he will take me with him, show me the way.

My husband goes back to his chair, my mother's hand is on my arm. "I *saw* the dessert," she tells me with a smile, "—Floating Island."

"It's not up to yours," I tell her, aware again of the party, the other guests. "The custard wanted to separate, the meringue wouldn't stand up high enough."

My mother helps me set out the dessert plates with hand-painted birds that were *her* mother's. Soon, we are all seated again. Although unable to consume the main course, I find that the sweet, thick yellow custard with its egg white meringue tastes good to me. As I scrape the bottom of my bowl, my father tells me how much he has enjoyed it, my father-in-law nods assent.

Then, as I sip the coffee my mother has poured into her favorite demitasse cups, I begin to feel weak, afraid. I imagine I am standing on a beach where the tide is going out. Wet sand is slipping away beneath my bare, chilled feet.

I have made a mistake. Why have I been talking about what happened after *their* lives ended? Why haven't I questioned them about the significance, the details of events *I* barely remember, or, which happened before I was born?

There are things I want to know, things that might explain, help me understand why I have—

Too late, too late—the dead are leaving—

"Oh Daddy," I beg like a child being put to bed early, "don't go, *please* don't go."

My mother rises. "We must—" she tells me.

My mother has my right hand, my father has my left. I am poised between them, small and uncertain.

The others are turning away. I want to give my husband a final kiss, but he is moving into the shadows. Looking back over his shoulder, he gives me a long look of farewell. My mother-in-law waves and smiles. Her eyes, as always, are dark.

"*Wait*," I call, but I can no longer see their faces. Their forms are merging into a grey, porous, after sunset mist. There is a faint, fresh smell of salt. I don't hear the front door open and close, but the draft makes the burned-down candles flicker. The salt smell is stronger. It makes me cough.

How long have I been standing here, watching the flames of the candles die down, rise again? One by one, they go out. Only one left. I should turn on the overhead lights.

Instead, I face the sideboard, stare down at what remains of the roast. I stare at the graining of the flesh, the unevenness of the edges of the few remaining slices, the browned softness of the cream-colored fat. I stare at the pale, yellowish bones.

Flesh, feathers, fur, scales, shells, bark. All living things have coverings—of one sort or another. How is it then to be uncovered, revealed? Is the formless remainder absorbed into something brilliant, perhaps a shadowless sea?

Mindlessly, I stare at the indented tree pattern of the silver platter. The tree is meant to carry the blood to the oval well at its root. The blood in the well has cooled, darkened. It is spotted with congealing islands of fat.

Idly, I poke a finger into the well, then suck it. It does not taste as I expect. Rather than hearty and succulent, it is thin and bitter.

Then, taking a white round of bread, I at first circle the well, and finally, dip into it. I consume that piece, then soak another, moving the crust in concentric circles, ever smaller. Now, apart from a slight glaze of fat, the well is empty, and in it, blurred but recogniz-able, is my own face.

The last candle is out. Its smoke is acrid. I turn on the lights. The room seems cold. I imagine I can see my own breath.

I must do the dishes, put the leftovers away. Sliding one palm under each end, I lift the oval platter. In my upturned wrists, the pulses throb.

The phone in the kitchen is ringing. I hurry in and set the

platter down. My daughter calling.

"What are you doing?" she asks.

"I had some guests," I explain vaguely, aware of the beating of my heart. "They've gone," I add, hoping she won't ask more.

"Oh—I was thinking of dropping by—"

"Do," I tell her. "There's roast beef left over if you want some."

The Bush

Old men get foolish. They tell stories that don't make sense.
I'm an old man, but my story isn't foolish. The trouble is: it isn't
sensible. To that I say back: not everything that happens *is* sensible.
This story is an example of that truth. No made-up nonsense can
hold a candle to it: so listen.

If it wasn't that a bush—the biggest in the county, many said
—once grew at the center of the green of this village, there would
be no story. There *was* such a bush—it stood where the stone fountain is now—though few remember it.

How the bush got to be the size it was, I don't know. It was a
cynosure from when I first remember it. When people gathered at the
green for parades, concerts or preachers, they would set their folding
chairs in the orb of the bush's shade, and the children would crawl
in under and play around the roots, hidden and happy.

The bigness of the bush didn't depend on its leaves: they were
nothing but small, dull-green ovals with pale-branching veins. The
bush's greatness came from its ever-so-long, spindly, waving-every-
which-way branches. There were hundreds and hundreds of those
thin, dun-colored branches—some stretching up sky high to show
they might grow forever, but then, when they got there, bowing
gracefully to gravity and bending, bending, bending back down to the
earth from where they had come.

In spring, the ends of the bush's branches bore the tiniest little
five-petaled flowers you ever saw—pink and sweet on the outside
and white and private within. Come fall, those flowers closed, hard-
ened and turned into clusters of snow-white berries. When winter
began, the white berries softened, fell and buried themselves in the
snow. In each berry, there were seeds so the bush could begin again.

I was in my prime then—I was the chief of the crew that did the work of the village's Highways and Parks department. My three boys were little, and my seven grandchildren, naturally, weren't born. We were mainly road men, but there weren't as many roads as now because not so many farm fields had been made into developments.

The green, same as now, was the only park in the village unless you wanted to count the cemetery, which was taken care of by an association with the churches, not by us. We put flowers around the Civil War monument at the north end of the green before Memorial Day, mowed all summer and painted the old iron and plank benches when they needed it. When the snows came, we cleared the walks— one north-south and the other east-west—and the ring path in the center that circled the high point of the park.

It was there, on a mound some said contained Indian artifacts, even bones, that the bush this story is about stood. That bush within the ring path at the walks' crossing was so big we didn't attempt to do much with it. We didn't go uphill underneath it with mowers; we didn't try to clip it back. We just let it do what it wanted, and what it wanted was—*to grow.*

Long before the bush burned by itself—yes, that's one part of what I'm telling that wars with sense—I had found out that the bush wasn't ordinary, apart from its size. It happened on a summer's afternoon when we were mowing. It was warm, but around the bush it was warmer still. I circumambulated, I checked. Like it or not, for a few feet out on all sides, there was something, you might have said an aura, of heat. It wasn't August four o'clock beside the bush: it was high noon.

I should have done something *then*, I suppose. I don't know what. But it was near quitting time and, just like now, I didn't enjoy the idea of making myself look foolish by telling what no one would believe. The long and the short of it was: I went home, ate the supper my wife Elysia had fixed—and forgot about it.

I don't think anyone else noticed the strangeness of the bush then, but when fall came, that changed. Maybe we were doing a last mowing of the green, maybe we were just raking leaves. Anyway, there was a chill in the wind, and several of the boys kept stopping by the bush. They felt the warmth. They joked about it. They said it was still summer there.

When we came next, to clear the first fall of snow from the walks, we came again to the ring path in the center. The bush, by then leafless, its white berries brown and shrunken, was warmer still. That time, awkward and sheepish with each other, we all admitted it.

Then, hesitating by the wonder with its great reservoir of branches rising and bending above our heads, we talked in whispers even though there was no one to hear us. Fevered, as it were, in the bush's aura, we contended with each other. One man was sure it was from something buried in the mound of earth. Another blamed sunspots. The last had read up on UFOs and discoursed thusly. I knew less than they did, but I kept my counsel. Suspicions were all I had.

Soon, we saw more of the bush's strangeness. Well before Thanksgiving, we all noticed that the bush didn't hold snow. Trees and bedding plants could be white and shrouded, branches loaded with cold weight, but, never mind that, the bush would be bare as bones. Dark and peculiar against the sky, that bush gushed up, reached out, spread wide, flowed far, fell, and rose again in a way that wasn't natural for a bush to do at all.

Then, early in December, we determined there was a *sound* that came from the bush, particularly at twilight. A tree, we all know, can be noisy. Branches scrape, leaves rustle, and sometimes, in a big storm, you hear trunks creak as they sway, ever so slightly.

The bush's sound—I almost said song, wasn't like any one of those things. It was high and quiet—like a young girl singing ever-so-softly to herself or maybe only humming. It was a carol that didn't have words, yet you could almost imagine them.

I guess I'd mentioned the bush to Elysia by that time. I don't know what the other fellows did, but you know how it is. Word gets around. Even before Christmas, people were beginning to take notice. I saw footprints in the snow inside the ring path. Beyond, underneath the branches, the ground seemed to be turning to warm mud.

Still, in this place—just a little village on the edge of a vast preserve of forests, lakes and wilderness—there wasn't anybody much to investigate. The December nights passed, one after another, and as it got nearer to Christmas, we all noticed how the bush glowed. The branches, same as before, were dark: no one had decked the bush with lights. What we saw shone from way underneath, kindled, as it were, by the roots.

Like anywhere else, people were busy with Christmas shopping and their own lives. What happened the night after Christmas, though, couldn't be ignored. It was that evening, shortly after sunset, that the bush set itself on fire.

Someone called the Fire Department, but that was hardly necessary as they are located at the far end of the green and could see for themselves. They hosed the fire out—it was dark by the time they finished—and that was all there was to it.

The next day, there was a three-paragraph story on the back page of the *County Observer* next to ads for after-Christmas sales. It said there had been a "conflagration" and blamed it on vandals.

What the article *didn't* say, and what no one else seemed to notice either, was the fact—true whether or not you believe it—that the bush, with all its upward-reaching and downward-returning branches, was the same before the fire as after. There were some grey ashes scattered underneath on the warm mound of mud—ashes that might have come from the burning of the bush's already fallen leaves. Otherwise, not one dark branch or twig had been consumed. Instead, strong against the winter sky, the bush stood inviolate.

Besides the leaf ashes though, there was one evidence that the fire had happened. It was a faint, smoky smell, but it wasn't the smell of burned wood. Instead, it was aromatic. It was a faint odor of incense, even perfume.

The second time the bush caught fire was the next-to-last day of the year. It happened to be a Friday. Again, it was twilight; again, everyone was hurrying somewhere—this time, for the New Year's weekend. The Fire Department came right away; they put the fire out. Only a few stopped to watch, and there was no article in the Saturday paper. As before, the bush was not consumed.

Then came a Sunday early in January. The bush burned again; the Fire Department came again. What was different that time was: they couldn't put the fire out.

It wasn't twilight; it was the middle of a chill, sunny day. People were coming out of the churches by the green; it was the time some call Epiphany, the time of the star. Naturally, a crowd gathered.

I'd stayed home that morning, but I heard the commotion, smelled the aromatic burning. We only live a couple of blocks from there, so I told Elysia and the boys to dress up warm—it was below freezing—and we walked over.

What we saw when we got there was the like of what I'll never see again. It was a skyward column of fire. The flames towered up from the mound where the bush grew, or maybe, from deep within the earth. For that jet, the bush wasn't much more than a complicated candlestick. The fire, we all said, was higher than the highest steeple.

Was cold the reason the fire wouldn't be put out? One hose froze. Another burst. Still, even when they did get water to the flames, the water didn't work.

Finally, a Fire Department from up in the woods got there. Elysia went home about that time—she had a chicken in the oven—but the boys and I stayed. Those men were used to blazing forests: they had some kind of chemicals. They snuffed the torrent of flame as if it had been a match. The fire didn't die *down*, it *died*.

Later, after supper, Elysia and I strolled back by ourselves. The sun had gone: it was zero-degrees, or less. The green, which looked like a messed-up ice rink from all the water, was deserted. Icicles hung like left-over stalactites from trees and telephone wires; they even looped down between the boards of park benches. The Civil War

monument could have been marble instead of granite: the ice sheath-
ing the obelisk was glistening and pearly.

The oddest-appearing thing of all was the bush itself. Ringed
by glassy ice piled near a foot deep, the bush still stood high and
strong on its mound with its nonsensical, every-which-way branches
silhouetted against a greyish yellow, after-sunset sky. Something,
though, was different.

We were standing in the street, which I'd had some of my boys
sand on Sunday overtime, and we weren't about to trek in over the
turbulent ice ridges and perilous ice troughs that covered the dried
grass of summer. Still, we could see that the strange branches of the
strange bush weren't dull and dark as they had been. The fire was
over, but those branches were bright as blazes. In truth, they
appeared to be turned to gold.

Now there are several places this story could end. This is one
of them. I could put in something about "ice glare" or "after-sunset
glow" and be done with it. Why not get out when the getting is
good?

Elysia would like that. Why go on about what's past, she says,
when they won't believe you anyway?

Being old doesn't have to mean being quiet, I say. She just
shakes her head, coughs, makes her way upstairs. I know what she's
thinking: she's thinking about *questions*—the ones I can't answer.

So if *you* want to know whether the bush's branches were
really gold, and if so, *why*, stop here. *I don't know.* What I do know
is what happened next.

It was only this: both of us saw, neither of us believed. Still,
shivering and shaking, we stood staring at what looked like fourteen
—even eighteen—carats. By then, there was only a little light left.
If that was what caused what appeared to our eyes, another part of
the twilight's deception was the way the golden bush seemed to contain what couldn't possibly be within its wondrous, glowing branches.

Elysia admitted to me that she saw a tall, dark man with gold
around his head. I admitted to her that I saw two pale men of royal

mien. Their crowns, of course, were the golden branches.

After we'd said those things, there was frost in our mouths, our ears, our noses. The cold, some might have surmised, was addling our brains. You can say that too if you like to think everything we see is sensible.

In any case, we weren't foolish enough to freeze to death gaping. We went home, and it was a good thing. Elysia was having trouble with her toes, the little ones, which had always been weaker than the others. Frostbite. The kids were in bed, but I lit a fire in the fireplace just for us, and I rubbed those toes until they came around and looked pink. All the while I rubbed, and even when the fire burned low, we didn't mention the bush again. Pretty soon, we went to bed. We weren't old then. We knew what to do with ourselves on a cold night.

The next morning early, driving to work, I learned what we'd seen wasn't twilight twaddle. The bush had been seen by others—not viewers but doers. For the great bush, which we'd left the night before standing like a tantalus on its rutted river mound of ice, wasn't there any more. That bush had been harvested by many hands, plucked to nothing. With the sun not up more than an hour, there wasn't a twig left.

What I heard after was: word about the golden bush had gone around in the night. Long before sunrise, there had been people scaling the slippery mound and sliding into each other. They had come with scissors, knives, and even axes and chain saws, but those who'd been there weren't telling. There was silly talk going around about the gold of the Magi, but if any of the people with frostbitten fingers got rich, we never saw signs of it afterwards.

Later, some of the few who would own up to it said the golden branches melted in their hands. Others, denying that, said the branches burned like dry ice, leaving long, festering infections in people's palms. The wildest tale of all claimed that even the tiniest wigs plucked could root themselves and grow to be bushes that would live longer than a man, maybe forever.

Senseless as such talk was, some believed it. Me and my men from Highways, we didn't bother to argue. We weren't being paid to philosophize; we were being paid to work, and that's just what we did. When the January thaw came, we filled in the cold cavity where the bush had been. Come spring, we decided, we would plant another kind of bush—a small one that wouldn't cause trouble.

There was wisdom in what we did, but what happened after-wards was preposterous. The cavity wouldn't stay filled. It absorbed good dirt; it stayed sunken. By the time the spring rains came, it was beginning to be a well. It wasn't a dug well, of course, it was a well in the sense that dark water kept welling up. If you looked into it, you couldn't see bottom. What you did see was the way the water kept spiraling and gurgling.

It got so you could *hear* the well, even before you came to the center of the green. The never-still, rising and rippling water made the whispery, swirling-on-itself sound that springs like to make. Just as the bush had made its music, the spring had a song all its own.

After Easter, we decided the only sensible thing: we would let the spot be what it was. When the ground unfroze, we set out to build a fountain. Since it was to be in the center of the green, the fountain had to look like something. Stone was suitable, but with money tight, as usual, we knew we couldn't get Civil War marker granite. So we compromised. We used stone, yes, but it was just *rocks* we got and hauled there.

After cementing a great round basin at the top of the mound, we cut and fitted those rocks as neatly as we could on the outside of it. It wasn't perfect, but it gave a rustic effect.

The problem that developed was that our fountain, such as it was, kept overflowing. It was more than spring rains; it was pressure growing from deep in the ground. To take care of that, we decided to carry the water further up where it seemed to want to go. We devised a pipe that let the water rise to a second, smaller basin set above the first. From up there—almost as high as the bush had been

—the water plashed down again and bubbled.

Being carried up high eased the water. The big bowl didn't overflow anymore unless it rained unusually heavy. For Memorial Day, we set petunias and geraniums all around it. People were pleased. Even Elysia, always one to have doubts, said it looked pretty.

As I've said, a story has to end some place. The trouble is: when the story is true and not made-up, things go on happening. Just like a fountain, they keep flowing.

Our fountain, by the way, still stands. One of the rocks didn't stay cemented, but nobody notices. It just sits where it fell. The big basin and the little one above it stay full. The only new thing is that the new Highways and Parks men have set bushes underneath around the mound. I suppose they thought bushes would be easier than petunias and geraniums every year. They might have made a mistake though, because those little bushes are the same kind as the big one that once grew there. Probably they'd heard that snow-berries grow fast.

My crew is all gone or retired, so there was no one to warn them, but even if I'd known before they did it, I don't think I'd have butted in. You can't go back and be what you were, and you can't tell people things that aren't sensible and expect them to pay attention, especially if you're old. When you're old, what you can mostly do is: wait.

I'm getting tired—maybe you are too—but there are two true things I have to add. *First*: To this day, the water rising in that fountain is fresh and good. People still stop to drink it; sometimes they fill jugs. *Second*: There are certain ones—I'm not going to name names—who claim the water makes them *feel* good, almost like wine. There are others who say the water has made them feel better.

By that I mean people like the woman from one of the churches who claimed drinking the water didn't just give her a remission— she called it a cure. Lately, I've been telling Elysia, who's been coughing more than she should, to try it. She says she will, but she hasn't. I say, being old isn't so bad: while there's life, there's hope.

She says: "Don't babble."

She means: don't run on like the fountain. So I stop. Pretty much, I do what she says. This morning though, I did something I didn't tell her. While she was doing the dishes, I slid out the side door. I had a jug, and I hiked to the fountain and filled it. Later, when she wasn't in the kitchen, I set the jug on the shelf by the sink. She's been in there since; I know she saw it. She knows I know, but neither of us will say it. I imagine she's guessed where the water came from too.

Just now, when she went upstairs slow and stumbling, I sneaked out to the kitchen again. What I did was: I took down an old white cup left from the set we had when we were first married and couldn't afford better. I knew more than to take a *good* cup she could complain about. That cup has crackles inside, and its handle was knocked off a long time ago. I didn't touch anything else, even though she hadn't yet wiped away the crumbs and the seeds of the rolls we'd had for breakfast—a thing that wouldn't have happened when she was well.

Now I'm just going to sit here and rest my eyes by closing them until she has to come down to fix lunch. My story ends as it began, with plain facts: an old cup with water in it, bread crumbs—and scattered seeds. That's enough, isn't it?

What more do you want?